Calvin Miller

THE

SINGER

TRILOGY

The Mythic Retelling

of the Story of the New Testament

THE SINGER,

THE SONG, THE FINALE

IN ONE VOLUME

Cover and interior illustrations
by Joe DeVelasco

INTERVARSITY PRESS
DOWNERS GROVE, ILLINOIS 60515

InterVarsity Press is the book-publishing division of InterVarsity Christian Fellowship, a student movement active on campus at hundreds of universities, colleges and schools of nursing in the United States of America, and a member movement of the International Fellowship of Evangelical Students. For information about local and regional activities, write Public Relations Dept., InterVarsity Christian Fellowship, 6400 Schroeder Rd., P.O. Box 7895, Madison, WI 53707-7895.

ISBN 0-8308-1321-7 (pbk.)

Printed in the United States of America ∞

Library of Congress Cataloging-in-Publication Data

Miller, Calvin.
    The singer trilogy: a mythic retelling of the story of the New
Testament/Calvin Miller; cover and interior illustrations by Joe
DeVelasco.
        p.   cm.
    Contents: The singer—The song—The finale.
    ISBN 0-8308-1300-4
    I. Title.
PS3563.I376S52   1990
811'.54—dc20   90-39944
                                                  CIP

14   13   12   11   10   9   8
03   02   01

THE
SINGER

1

For most who live,
hell is never knowing
who they are.
The Singer knew and
knowing was his torment.

When he awoke, the song was
there.

Its melody beckoned and begged
him to sing it.

It hung upon the wind and
settled in the meadows where
he walked.

He knew its lovely words and
could have sung it all, but
feared to sing a song whose
harmony was far too perfect for
human ear to understand.

And still at midnight it
stirred him to awareness, and
with its haunting melody it
drew him with a curious mystery
to stand before an open window.

In rhapsody it played among the
stars.

It rippled through Andromeda
and deepened Vega's hues.

It swirled in heavy strains
from galaxy to galaxy and gave
him back his very fingerprint.

"Sing the Song!" the heavens
seemed to cry. "We never
could have been without the
melody that you alone can
sing."

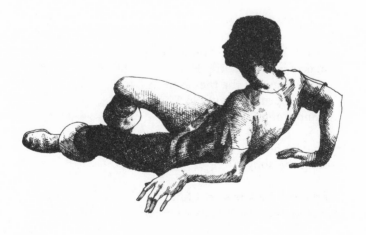

But he drew back, sighing
that the song they so
desired was higher than the earth.

And always in his agony of
longing and reluctance, the
atmosphere around him argued
back.

"You, too, are higher than the
earth! You sang the higher
music once, before the oceans
ever crashed their craggy
coasts."

He braced himself upon a
precipice above the canyon floor,
and with the wind full on his
face, he cried into the sky:

  "Earthmaker, tell me
  if I have the right
  to sing..."

But then his final word trailed
off into gales.

The gull screamed.

"No," he thought, "only Earthmaker is everlasting. His
alone must be the theme from
which sprung the world I
stand upon."

And so he only loved but never
sang the song.

Full well he knew that few
would ever see him as a singer

of so grand a piece.

He knew that they would say to
him:

"You are no singer! And even
if you are you should sing the
songs we know."

And well he knew the penalty of
law. A dreamer could be ostracized
in hate for singing songs the
world had never heard.

Such songs had sent a thousand
singers to their death already.

And the song which dogged his
aching steps and begged him
pleadingly to sing it was
completely unfamiliar.

Only the stars and mountains
knew it. But they were old. And
man was new, and chained to
simple, useless rhymes; thus he
could not understand the majesty
that settled down upon him.

But daily now it played upon his
heart and swept his soul, until
the joy exploded his awareness—
crying near the edge of sanity,
"Sing... sing... S I N G!"

II

It is strange how
oftentimes the air
speaks.

We are sane as long
as we hear voices
when there are none.

We are insane when
we hear nothing and
worse we are deaf.

He worked the wood and drove
the pegs methodically.

The shavings from the adze
piled high upon the floor.

"Earthmaker, full of mercy,"
he said, when evening had
come, "I am a tradesman!"

"No," said the silent air,
"not a tradesman—a troubadour instead!"

"A tradesman!" he said firmly
as he smashed his mallet on
the vise.

"A troubadour!" the silence
thundered back.

III

Two artists met one time within
a little wood. Each brought
his finest painting stroked by
his complete uniqueness. When
each revealed his canvas to the
other—they were identical.

So once in every solar system
there are two fingerprints alike.

But only once.

His seeming madness made the
music play a hundred times
more loudly than before.

It lured him from his highland
home.

He left the mallet broken on
the vise and walked away.

Never had he been the way he
walked, and yet his feet knew
every step. He could not cease
to marvel how they moved his
body forward through the
mist of circumstances which he
vaguely knew by name.

His naked feet intrigued him,
for they moved with purpose
which his mind had not yet
measured. Besides they each
one wore a curious scar of some
wound as yet unopened; yet they
had been there long before his
birth. What twist of meaning
had Earthmaker given him, to
scar his feet before he ever
walked?

From the hills, he walked ever
downward to the valley miles
below.

Down, down, down—until the
vegetation thickened into
shrubs, and the desert gave

way to river jungles.

And there where water lapped
at his fatigue, he heard a
singer, singing his compelling
carols to the empty air.

The tradesman knew that it was just
an earth song, for it was
different from the Star-Song
which begged him be its singer—
yet somehow like it.

The River Singer finished and
they walked into the trees.

"Are you the Troubadour, who
knows the Ancient Star-Song?"
the tradesman softly asked.

"No, *you* are the Great Troubadour
for whom the songless world,
so long has waited," the
River Singer said. "Sing, for many
years now, I have hungered
to hear the Ancient Star-Song . . ."

"I am a tradesman only . . ."

Then the River Singer waded out
into the water and beckoned
with his hand. Slowly
the tradesman followed.

They stopped waist-deep in
water. Their eyes swam and
they waited for the music
to begin.

It did.

The tradesman knew the River
Singer heard it too.

The water swirled around them
and the music surged.

Every chord seemed to fuse the
world in oneness.

They stood until the surging
current buried them in song.
It then receded and the music
died away.

And the river was once more a
simple river.

Then over that thin silver
stream the thunder pealed, and
a voice called from the sky
above . . .

"Tradesman! You are
the Troubadour! Go
now and sing!"

IV

I knew a blind man
whom a surgeon
helped to see. The
doctor never had a
lover such as he.
It is in such a way
that singers love
composers.

F rom the river, he moved on
and on in quietness alone.

He still talked to Earthmaker
as he always had but now he
called him "Father-Spirit."
He loved the newer name.

The Star-Song came upon him
with a manly joy.

At last he sang!

He threw the song against the
basalt canyon walls.

It ricocheted in splendor,
and he remembered far before
that he had sung those very
canyons into being.

"Father-Spirit!" he shouted
at the desert sky, "I love you.
Ask of me anything you will
and I will do it all."

The universe gathered up the
echoes of his joy and answered
back, "I love you, too, my
Singer. One thing alone I ask
of you:

   Sing my Ancient Star-
   Song to the world."

"Father-Spirit, I will sing it,
in every country will I sing

it, till all the world you love
can sing it."

In joy he sang and sang until
he fell asleep upon the desert
floor.

V

Hate sometimes
stands quite
close to love.

God too stands
often near to
evil—like si-
lent chessmen—
side by side.
Only the color
of the squares
is different.

H e was not alone when he awoke.

The ancient World Hater had
come upon his resting place
and not by chance.

The Hater leered at him with
one defiant, impish grin.

"Hello, Singer!"

"Hello, World Hater," the
Troubadour responded.

"You know my name, old friend
of man?"

"As you know mine, old enemy of
God."

"What brings you to the desert?"

"The Giver of the Song!"

"And does he let you sing it
only in these isolated spots?"

"I only practice here to sing it
in the crowded ways!"

It was hard to sing before the
World Hater, for he ground each
joyous stanza underneath his heel.

The music only seemed to make
the venom in his hate more
bitter than before.

The Hater drew a silver flute
from underneath his studded
belt. He placed it to his
leathered lips drawn tight to
play a melody.

The song surprisingly was
sweet. It filled the canyon
with an airy-tune and hung its
lingering reverberations myster-
iously in every cleft. It
rippled on the very ground
around their feet.

A strange compulsion came upon
the Singer. Furiously he wanted
so to sing the Hater's tune.

He barely staunched the eager
urge to sing.

The morning sun glinted fire
upon the silver flute. The music
and the dazzling light appeared
to mesmerize the Singer.

"You must not sing the Hater's
song," the Father-Spirit cried,
"Be very careful, for I love you,
Troubadour."

"Now," cried the World Hater,
"Let's do this tune at once.
I'll pipe, you sing. Think of
the thousand kingdoms that will
dance about our feet."

"No, Hater, I'll not sing your melodies,"
the Troubadour replied.

"What then Singer will you sing?"

"The Ancient Star-Song of the
Father-Spirit."

"Alone, without accompaniment?"

"Yes, Hater, all alone if need be."

"You need my pipe, man."

"You need my song instead."

"The music of your song is far
beyond my tiny pipe."

"Then, go! For I shall never sing
a lesser piece."

Then all at once the Troubadour
began again. The mountains
amplified his song. It swirled
as sunlit symphony, until
the Hater put his pipe beneath
his belt and fled before
the song of love.

"Beloved Singer, beware the
World Hater," the Father-Spirit said.

Then upward there the Singer
stretched his arms and said
again, "I love you, Father-Spirit."

He waited there a moment while
the sky embraced him and then
he walked away. Ahead he saw
the cities rise, and people
thronged the crowded ways.

VI

If she has loved
him, a man will
carry anything
for his mother—
a waterpot or a
world.

Where first to sing?" he
thought.

He turned back to the highlands where he had left the
broken tool so useless on the
vise.

For days he walked. The dust
flew up around his feet as he
walked home.

At length, he passed the village
signpost and there by odd
coincidence, his mother at
that very time stood by the
well.

They met.

He reached to carry her stone
jar.

"It's not traditional," she said.

He took it anyway.

Her cares had made her fifty
years seem even more.

"You broke your hammer on the
vise," she said. "I had it
mended for you."

"I'm through with hammers, anyway,"
he said. "I've just come home
to board the shop."

"And then you'll leave?"

"I will," he said.

"Where will you go?" She
studied paving stones as on they
walked. He moved the heavy jar
to ride upon his other shoulder.

"Wherever there are crowds of
many people."

"The Great Walled City of the
Ancient King?"

"Yes, I suppose."

He feared to talk to her. Yet
he must tell her of the River
Singer and all about the Star-
Song, he had so lately sung.
He seemed afraid that she would
think him mad. He could not
bear to hurt her. For besides
the Father-Spirit, he loved her
most of all. At length he knew
he must lay bare his heart.

"You seem so troubled, son," she
said.

"Not for myself," he said. Then
with the hand that was not needed
in balancing the jar, he took
her hand and smiled.

"I hate for you to board the
shop and leave..."

"Am I the tradesman that my father

was, while still he was alive?"
he asked.

"You both were good, but somehow
wood is never kind to your great
hands. Your father's hands never
paid the pain it cost you, just
to love his trade."

She looked down at the gentle,
suffering hand that held her own.
Somewhere in her swimming recol-
lection, she remembered the
same hand with infant fingers
that had clutched the ringlets of her
hair and reached to feel the
leathered face of Eastern Kings.
But he could not remember that.

They walked still further without
speaking.

"MOTHER, I AM THE SINGER!" He
blurted out at once.

"I know," she said.

"I love the Father-Spirit more
than life. He has sent me to
the crowded ways to sing the
Ancient Star-Song."

"I know," she said again. "I
heard the Ancient Star-Song
only once. It was the very
night that you were born. And
all these years, my son, I've
known that you would come to
board the shop someday. Can
you sing the Star-Song yet?"

"I can," he answered back.

They neared a house and entered.
They shared a simple meal
and sat in silence. And the song,
which they alone of all the world
did know, was lingering all
around them in the air.

She had not heard its strains
for thirty years but hungered for
its music.

He had not sung it for an afternoon but longed to have its
fluid meaning coursing through
his soul.

Of course the song began.

VII

Before the song all
music came like
muted, empty octaves
begging a composer's pen.
The notes cried silently
for paper staves and
kept their sound in theory only.

In the beginning was
the song of love.
Alone in empty nothingness
and space
It sang itself through
vaulted halls above
Reached gently out to
touch the Father's face.

And all the tracklessness
where worlds would be
Cried "Father" through the
aching void. Sound tore
The distant chasm, and eternity
Called back—"I love you Son—
sing Troubadour."

His melody fell upward
into joy
And climbed its way
in spangled rhapsody.
Earthmaker's infant stars
adored his boy,
And blazed his name through
every galaxy.

"Love," sang the Spirit Son
and mountains came.
More melody, and life
began to grow.
He sang of light, and darkness
fled in shame
Before a universe in
embryo.

Then on the naked ground
the Troubadour

Knelt down and firmly sang
  a stronger chord.
He scooped the earth dust
  in his hand
And worked the clay
  till he had molded man.

They laid him down beneath
  primeval trees
And waited there. They loved
  him while he slept
And both rejoiced as he began
  to breathe
A triumph etched in brutal
  nakedness.

"I am a Man!" the sun-crowned
  being sang.
He stood and brushed away the
  clinging sand.
He knew from where his very
  being sprang.
Wet clay still dripped from
  off the Singer's hands.

Earthmaker viewed the sculptured
  dignity
Of man, God-like and strident,
  President
Of everything that was,
  content to be
God's intimate and only earthen
  friend.

The three embraced in that
  primeval glen.
And then God walked away,
  his Singer too.
Hate came—discord—they
  never met again.

The new man aged and died
  and dying grew
A race of doubtful, death-owned
  sickly men.
And every child received the
  planet's scar
And wept for love to come and
  reign. And then
To heal hate-sickened life
  both wide and far.

"We're naked!" cried the
  new men in their shame.
  (they really were)
A race of piteous things
  who had no name.

They died absurdly whimpering
  for life.
They probed their sin for
  rationality.
Self murdered self in endless
  hopeless strife
And holiness slept with
  indecency.

All birth was but the prelude
  unto death
And every cradle swung above
  a grave.
The sun made weary trips from
  east to west,
Time found no shore, and
  culture screamed and raved.

The world, in peaceless orbits,
  sped along
And waited for the Singer and
  his song.

VIII

It is always much more
difficult to sing when
the audience has turned
its back.

The Singer ceased.

The Ancient Star-Song slept.

"You know the final verse?"
his mother asked.

"I know it all," he answered
back. "But I'll not sing it
here. I'll wait till I am on
the wall. Then alone the
melody will fall upon thick
ears."

"They will not like the final
verse," she said.

"They will not like it, for its
music is beyond their empty days
and makes them trade their
littleness for life."

"The self of every singer of the
song must die to know its music?"

"They all must die, and ever
does the self die hard. It
screams and begs in pity not to
go. Nor can it bear to let the
Father-Spirit own the soul."

He turned the thoughts methodically within his mind then spoke
again, "Mother, I shall sing the
song while I move out to seek
more singers who like me are
quite content to sing, then die."

She knew that he was right, but
found it hard to talk of joyous
life and painful death at the
same time. How odd the song born
on Earthmaker's breath should
lead his only Troubadour to death.

"I cannot bear to see you
   die. Let all
The world go by. Don't
   sing upon the wall.
At least don't sing the
   hell-bound ancient curse.
If you must sing of life
   leave off the final verse."

"I go," he said. "God give me
strength to sing upon the wall—
the Great Walled City of the
Ancient King."

He turned.

She cried.

"Leave off the final verse and
not upon the wall."

He kissed her.

"I can't ignore
   the Father-Spirit's call
So I will sing it there,
   and I will sing it all."

IX

A healthy child is
somehow very much
like God. A hurting
child, his son.

The sunlight lured him from the
shaded, village streets and drew
him into day. And everywhere
he went, the World Hater had
already been. The sick men lay
among the roadside thorns. The
old ones groaned from habit.
The young ones whimpered out of
hopelessness.

The Singer stopped. Beside the
road he saw a brown-eyed child.
Her mouth was drawn in hard,
firm lines that could not bend
to either smile or frown. Her
sickness ate her spirit, devouring
all the sparkle in her eyes.

Her legs misshapen as they were,
lay useless underneath the coarsest
sort of cloth. The Singer
knelt beside her in the dust and
touched her limpid hand and
cried. He drew the cloth away
that hid her legs. He reached
his calloused hand and touched
the small, misshapen foot.

"I too was born with scarred
feet. See mine!" he said,
drawing back the hem of his own robe.

She seemed about to speak, when
the music of a silver pipe broke
in the air around them. He had
heard the pipe before.

Above them towered the World
Hater.

"I knew you'd come," he said.
"You will, of course, make
straight her twisted limbs?"

"I will, World Hater . . . but can
you have no mercy? She's but a
child. Can her wholeness menace
you in any way? Would it so
embarrass you to see her skipping
in the sun? Why hate such
little, suffering life?"

"Why chide me, Singer? She's
Earthmaker's awful error. Tell
your Father-Spirit he should
take more time when he creates."

"No, it is love which brings a
thousand children into life in
health. It is hate that cripples
each exception to eternal joy.
But why must you forever toy
with nature to make yourself
such ugly pastimes of delight?"

"I hate all the Father-Spirit
loves. If he would only hate
the world with me, I'd find no
joy in it again. You sing.
The only music that I know is
the cacophony of agony that
grows from roadside wretches
such as these."

The child between them lay
bewildered by their conversation.
The Singer spoke again:

"I'll bring my song against
    your hate
Against the bonds of human
    sins.
And human tears will all subside
When the Ancient Star-Song wins."

The Hater raged and screamed
above his crippled joy:

"Sing health! If you must.
Sing everybody's but your own.
I soon will have your song,
likewise your life.
Your great Star-Song is
    doomed to fall.
You'll groan my kind
    of music
When I meet you at
    the wall."

The Singer scooped the frightened
child into his arms. He
sang and set her in the sunny
fields and thrilled to watch her
run. The world was hers in a
way she'd never known. The
butterfly-filled meadows danced
her eyes alive and drew her
scurrying away.

And others came!

Untouchables with bandages
heard the healing song and came
to health:

The crippled and the blind.
Sick of soul
Sick of heart

Sick of hate
Sick of mind.
Everywhere the music went, full health
came.

And all the way, men everywhere
were whispering that the long-
awaited Troubadour had come.

"It is he," they said, "at last
he's come. Praise the Father-
Spirit, he has come."

X

The word *crying*
does not appear
in the lexicon
of heaven. It
is the only word
listed in the
lexicon of hell.

The Singer woke at midnight.
In the stupor of half-
consciousness—neither quite
aware nor yet asleep—he was
alone.

The air was full of moans. With
groans of grief and pity, the
night was crying. He had never
heard the darkness cry before.

"Where are you, World Hater?" he
shouted.

"Standing in the doorway of the
worlds—reveling in my melodies
of ugliness and death."

The Singer listened. The morbid
air depressed him and he could
not help but weep himself. He
ached from the despair. "How long
have they cried beyond the doorway
of the worlds?" he asked.

The World Hater seemed to summon
up the volume of their moaning
and then he shouted, "They've
moaned a million years—
It never stops. They hurt with
pain that burns and eats the conscience—illuminating every
failure. They never can be free.
Crying is the only thing they
know."

"Poor souls! Have they nothing

to look back upon with joy?"
the Singer asked.

"No. Nor anything to look forward
to with hope."

"Could they never give up suffering
for one small moment, every
thousand years or so?"

"No. Never. They ache in simply
knowing they will never cease to
ache."

"I'm coming to the Canyon of the
Damned you know."

"You dare not think that you could
sing above their anguished dying
that never will be dead."

"You'll see, World Hater. I will
come."

"It's my domain!" the Hater protested.

"You have no domain. How dare
you think that you can hold some
corner of Earthmaker's universe
and make it your own private
horror chamber!"

"It is forever, Singer!"

"Yes, but not off-limits to the
song. I'll smash the gates that
hold the damned and every chain
will fall away.

"I'll sing to every suffering
cell of hate, the love song of
my soul.

"I'll stand upon the torment of
the Canyon of the Damned."

The troubled air grew still. The
World Hater stepped outside the
universe—pulled shut the doorway
of the worlds.

And Crying softly slept with Joy.

XI

Oftentimes Love is
so poorly packaged
that when we have
sold everything to
buy it, we cry in
finding all our
substance gone and
nothing in the tin-
sel and the ribbon.

Hate dresses well
to please a buyer.

He met a woman in the street. She leaned against an open door and sang through her half-parted lips a song that he could barely hear. He knew her friendship was for hire. She was without a doubt a study in desire. Her hair fell free around her shoulders. And intrigue played upon her lips.

"Are you betrothed?" she asked.

"No, only loved," he answered.

"And do you pay for love?"

"No, but I owe it everything."

"You are alone. Could I sell you but an hour of friendship?"

Deaf to her surface proposition, he said, "Tell me of the song that you were singing as I came upon you. Where did you learn it?"

His question troubled her. At length she said, "The first night that I ever sold myself, I learned it from a tall impressive man."

"And did he play a silver pipe?" the Singer asked.

She seemed surprised. "Do you

know the man who bought me
first?"

"Yes. Not long ago, in fact, he
did his best to teach that song
to me."

"I cannot understand. I sell
friendship and you your melody.
Why would he teach us both the
self-same song?"

The Singer pitied her. He knew
the World Hater had a way of making
every victim feel as though
he were the only person who
could sing his song.

"He only has one song; he therefore teaches it to everyone. It
is a song of hate."

"No, it is a love song. The first
night that he held me close, he
sang it tenderly and so in every
way he owned me while he sang
to me of love."

"And have you seen him since?"

"No, not him, but a never ending
queue of men with his desires."

"So it was no song of love. Tell
me, did he also say that some
day in the merchandising of your
soul, you would find someone who
would not simply leave his fee
upon the stand but rather take
you home to care for you and

cherish you?"

Again she seemed surprised, "Those
were indeed his very words—how
can you know them?"

"And have you found the one that
he has promised?"

"Not yet."

"And how long have you peddled
friendship?"

"Some twenty years are gone since
first I learned the song that you
inquired about."

The Singer felt a burst of pity.
"We sometimes give ourselves
to hate in masquerade and only
think it love. And all our lives
we sing the song we thought
was right. The Canyon of the Damned
is filled with singers who
thought they knew a love song...
Listen while I sing for you
a song of love."

He began the melody so vital
to the dying men around him.
"In the beginning was the song of
love..."

She listened and knew for the
first time she was hearing all of
love there was. Her eyes swam
when he was finished. She sobbed
and sobbed in shame. "Forgive me,
Father-Spirit, for I am sinful

and undone... for singing weary
years of all the wrong words..."

The Singer touched her shoulder
and told her of the joy that lay
ahead if she could learn the
music he had sung.

He left her in the street and
walked away, and as he left he
heard her singing his new song.
And when he turned to wave the
final time he saw her shaking
her head to a friendship buyer.
She would not take his money.

And from his little distance,
the Singer heard her use his
very words.

"Are you betrothed?" the buyer
asked her.

"No, only loved," she answered.

"And do you pay for love?"

"No, but I owe it everything."

XII

In hell there is no music—
an agonizing night that
never ends as songless as
a shattered violin.

S ing the Hillside Song!" they
cried.

There were so many of them. He
wasn't even sure he could be
heard above the din of all their
voices. He walked among them
and looked them over. In his
mind he knew that the Father-Spirit
wanted each of them to learn
his song.

Someone in the sprawling crowd
stood and handed him a lyre.
"Sing for us please Singer—the
Hillside Song!"

"Yes, yes," they called, "the Hillside Song."

He looked down at the lyre and
held it close. He turned each
thumbset till the string knew
how to sound, then he began:

"Blessed are the musical," he
said, "for theirs shall be a
never-ending song."

"Blessed are those who know the
difference between their loving
and their lusting, for they shall
be pure in heart and understand
the reason."

"Blessed are those who die for
reasons that are real, for they
themselves are real."

"Blessed are all those who yet
can sing when all the theater
is empty and the orchestra is gone."

"Blessed is the man who stands
before the cruelest king and
only fears his God."

"Blessed is the mighty king who
sits beside the weakest man and
thinks of all their similarities."

"Earthmaker is love. He has sent
his only Troubadour to close
the Canyon of the Damned."

Then they broke his song and cried
out with one voice, "Tell us
Singer, have you any hope for us?
Can we be saved?"

"You may if you will sing Earthmaker's Song!"

"Is there another way to cheat
the Canyon of the Damned?"

"None but the Song!"

XIII

No person ever is so helpless as
the man in whom joy and misery
sleep comfortably together.

No physician can give health and
happiness to the man who enjoys
his affliction. For such a man
health and happiness are always
contradictory.

From night to day and back to
night again he travelled on.
He saw the glow of the great city,
far on the horizon, and just
the light of it roused expectancy
and fear. By twilight he was
weary and he turned aside to
sleep beside a moonlit stream.
The water fell in froth and white
cascades into the wooden lattice
of a creaking wheel.

The Miller who was still at work
seemed most determined to finish
out his toil by starlight. It
was only by the merest chance he
found the Singer sleeping by the
stream just above the giant wheel.

For a moment he saw the Singer only
as a vagrant and was inclined to
drive him from the premises. But
then he changed his mind and
invited him to share the evening
meal.

As they went into the grain room,
the Singer looked upon the great
machine which turned the giant
stones which milled the grist.

The Singer was about to ask him
where he found the mason to
quarry such impressive stones,
when suddenly he discovered that
one of the Miller's hands was
badly scarred and crippled.

"Can you run so great a stone
with but a single hand?" The
Singer asked.

"I manage . . . though it always was
much easier with two."

"Did you lose your hand in this
machinery?"

"I was in much too great a hurry
three harvest-times ago. I was
trying to sweep the grist away
when I dropped my broom upon the
floor stone. When I reached to
pick it up, the great stone caught
my arm and hand. And when they
rolled the grinder back, this was
all that I had left," he said.

"I will," observed the Singer,
"make it useful once again if you
will just desire it whole and
believe it can be."

"It cannot be so easy, Singer.
Would you wave your magic wand
above such suffering and have it
all be done with? I sometimes
wake at midnight with a searing
flame of fire and throbbing
agony alive through all this
twisted, dying limb. You have
both hands and cannot understand
this sort of pain."

"I have no pain like yours, but
I have a healing melody. Earthmaker gave the song to me for
healing hands like yours.

Already it has helped a little
girl to be made whole."

"Was her hand as badly mangled
as my own?"

"It was her legs—but yes, they
were..."

"How often I have wished that I
might trade a useless hand for such
a leg," the Miller interrupted.

"Why either—why not simply be
made whole?"

"Oh that such a healing now were
possible—the speed I might regain
in working at the mill. But no, it
cannot be. Can you not understand? Have you no sympathy
for suffering? Are you so
empty of conscience as to suggest
a hopeless remedy. You only add
to misery by forcing me to see
myself a cripple. I soon shall
have to close the mill or sell it.
I cannot make the necessary
quota since the accident occurred."

"There is power within the Melody
I know to make you well. Please,
Miller, trust and let me sing and
you will run the mill alone
with two good hands."

"Stop your mocking. I am a
sick old man whom life has cheated
of a hand. The nightly pain has
already now begun. The season

of my hope is gone."

The Singer watched him caught in
some dread spasm of his aching circumstance. He moaned and fell
upon the floor and with his healthy
fingers he held his mangled hand.

His surging pain caused him to
cry, "O God deliver me from this
body . . . I never can be well
and whole as other men."

He waited for the Singer to join
him in his pity, but when he
raised his head for understanding,
the door stood open on the night
and the Singer was nowhere to
be seen.

XIV

To God obscenity is not uncovered
flesh. It is exposed intention.
Nakedness is just a state of heart.
Was Adam any more unclothed when
he discovered shame? Yes.

The wall of the great city reached
upward till it defied all measurement
of mind.

Outside the fortress, stretching
up the slopes, a grove of trees
bearded the great stone wall that
had slept for centuries above the seasons
of new leaf and naked frost.

Towers and minarets glinted
in the sun-washed sky and caused
the Singer apprehension as he
leaned against a tree.

He watched the human commerce flow-
ing through the rough-hewn gates.
Never had he seen so many people
hungry for a living song. They
jostled shapelessly, a mass of urban
sameness. Each hurried after
urgent unattended business, yet
none had any reason for the press.

The Singer sighed.

Sometimes a child would follow in
the madding throng. Already it
appeared the youngster tried to
learn the routine, manufactured steps
of older men he mimicked in the way.

Reluctant to adopt the business
cadence of the empty throng,
the Singer turned and sought a quiet
place beneath the wall. He walked
into the trees.

"Hello, Singer," said the voice he
knew too well. "Welcome to the
quiet of the grove. Does the
senseless empty crowd offend you?"

The Singer's only offense came in
knowing that the World Hater always
seemed to know what he was thinking.

"How did you manage to make them
cherish all this nothingness?"
he asked the World Hater.

"I simply make them feel embarrassed
to admit that they are incomplete. A
man would rather close his eyes than
see himself as your Father-Spirit
does. I teach them to exalt their
emptiness and thus preserve the
dignity of man."

"They need the dignity of God."

"You tell them that. I sell a
cheaper product."

They were deeper in the woods.
They stopped in a shaded spot
beneath the fortress wall.

A heavy set of chains hung from
a great foundation stone that
held the towering wall. Manacles
hung bolted on the wrists of a
burly, naked man.

He slept or seemed to.

Before him on the ground lay a
heavy stoneware basin nearly

filled with water and the dried
remains of bread half-eaten.

"Is he mad?" the Singer asked.

"Senselessly," the Hater answered.

"Who brings him bread and water?"

"I do."

"Why?"

"To see him dance in madness
without a tiny hope! Imagine my
delight when he raves and screams
in chains. Would you like for me
to wake this animal?"

"He is a man. Earthmaker made him
so. What is his name?"

"The Crowd."

"Why such a name?"

"Because within this sleeping hulk
there are a thousand hating spirits
from the Canyon of the Damned. They
leap at him with sounds no ears but
his can hear. They dive at him with
screaming lights no other eyes can
see. And in his torment he will
hold his shaggy head and whimper.
Then he rises and strains in fury
against the chains to tear them
from the wall. Stand back and see."

The Hater took the silver pipe out
of its sheath. The tune began—a

choppy, weird progression of half
tones.

The sleeping giant stirred and placed
his massive hands upon his temples.
In fever hot the Hater played and just
as rapidly the Madman stumbled to his
feet.

The Singer never had beheld so
great a man as he. Some unseen,
unheard agony rippled through
his bleeding soul. He growled,
then screamed and tried to tear the
chains that held him to the wall.

"Stop, Hater!" cried the Singer.

But the Hater played more loudly
than before. At that precise and
ugly moment, the pinion on the left
gave way. The chain fell loose.
Then with his one free hand the monster
tore the other chain away. In but
a second he stood unchained
before them. The Hater took his
pipe and fled into the trees. The
Singer then began to sing and
continued on until the Madman stood
directly in his path. With love
that knew no fear, the Singer
caught his torment, wrapped it all
in song and gave it back to him as
peace.

And soon the two men held each other.
In their long embrace of soul, the
spirits cried and left. They
stood at last alone.

"What year is it?" the giant asked
with some perplexity.

"It is the year of the Troubadour,"
the Singer said. "How long have
you hung upon the wall and writhed
in madness?"

"I cannot tell the years."

"Will you come with me into the
ancient city?"

"Yes," said the Madman, and then
remembering, he added, "I cannot,
for I am naked."

"Not if you love me. He whom
Earthmaker loves," replied the
Troubadour, "is hidden from his
shame forevermore."

"I love you more than life," the
Madman then confessed.

And when they turned to leave the
two of them were dressed.

XV

Humanity is fickle.
They may dress for a
morning coronation and
never feel the need to
change clothes to
attend an execution in
the afternoon.

So Triumphal Sundays
and Good Fridays
always fit comfortably
into the same April
week.

The way through the gates was full.
The Holiday had come and the
eagerness of all the citizens for
tradition and festivity had charged
the air with expectation. The
Singer and the Madman felt the strain
of something dread but pending,
threatening but unannounced.

Within the press of people the Singer
felt a mixing of compassion and
revulsion. He pitied them for
emptiness but resented their contentment in it. He knew that what
they needed was the Song.

When they approached the gates, a
woman in the crowd came to the
Madman, then shuddering fell
back in fright. They stopped and
the congestion moved around
them.

"You are the Madman," she said.
Then changing her mind she denied
it, "No you are clothed and sane."

"I am the Madman," he said, "but the
Troubadour has come and I am full
and whole."

"Who is this Troubadour?" she asked.

"He is the Son of Earthmaker!"

A crowd was gathering around
their conversation.

"Listen to me," called the
Madman to the crowd.

"I hung upon the wall until
this very hour. When the moon
was full I roamed in wild
unholy grottoes of my mind. See
these wrists," he said pulling
back his sleeves.

The marks and scars of chafing
steel were obvious to all.

"The manacles of iron did this.
I could kill and would have
many times except for the great
chains which held me. I cried
within the grove and wished to
die. I tore at every band and
tried to set my own brutality
toward freedom, but never did the
chains give way until today."

"Stop!" cried a voice within the
crowd. "You are still mad," the
voice continued as the Hater
came out of the crowd. "Listen
to me, Madman," he said pulling
out the silver pipe.

Beads of perspiration appeared
upon the Madman's brow. Fear
tore at him—could he stand
the melody that formerly had
driven him insane? The weird
progression of shrieking notes
began.

But the Madman's tension soon
began to ease. In the frustration

of his losing, the Hater played
more loudly than before.

Soon the Madman was entirely at
peace. He exulted in the confidence of total sanity. "It's
no use Hater, the Troubadour has
come."

The crowd had grown to several
hundred people and the Madman
called out over them, "This
man's pipe wiped out all my
sanity until today. I learned a
new song from the Singer for whom
the world so long has waited.
Listen to the Song of Life."

He began to sing. The Singer
himself was startled at the beauty
of his voice. He sang with such
confidence that none could doubt
the meaning he found springing up
within his soul.

"Where did you learn this confidence and joy?" they asked him.

He nodded toward the Singer.
"He has saved me from myself
and from a thousand maddened spirits
from the Canyon of the Damned."

"Who are you, Man?" they asked the
Singer.

"I am the Troubadour, the Son of
Earthmaker," the Singer then
replied. "I have come
to save the world and close

the Canyon of the Damned."

"Can we know your saving song
and sing it as the Madman does?"

"You may, if you believe I
am the only Troubadour."

They mulled the proposition
in their muddled minds.

Then someone in the fringe cried
loudly, "Halana to the Troubadour,
Son of Earthmaker!" Another to the
far left took up the cry. A third
and then a fourth—and suddenly
the world seemed caught up in the
cry.

"Halana to the Troubadour,
Earthmaker's only Son."

Through the ancient city gates the joy
echoed down the plaster canyons and
drubbed its cadence over cobblestones.
The cry became a tumult in the city,
   Joy to the Earth,
   The Troubadour has come
   Make ready for the Song of Life.

A thousand dancers swelled the streets
and instruments of music gathered up
the merriment of holiday. Every
street cried out the newness of the
singing age that came to close
the joyless era that had gone before.

The music swept through every city street
and purged the evil and the sin
before it. The Hater dropped his

pipe and barely could retrieve it
from beneath the thousand driving feet.

The Song had come, and for one
swelling surge of love there was
no room for hate.

Even the sentinels upon the
walls raised their hands, threw their
bearded faces to the sky and cried
out over all the world beneath them,
"Halana to the Troubadour,
Earthmaker's only Son."

XVI

SYLLOGISM

Major Premise:
God is a custom.

Minor Premise:
A custom is an
old, old habit.

Conclusion:
Therefore, God is
an old, old habit.

The singing and the dancing swept
the crowd in joyful madness till
all the city gathered in the
Plaza of Humanity—a colonnaded
forum around the Shrine of Older Life.

The Shrine of Older Life was
attended by the Keepers of the
Ancient Ways. They were every
one gray-bearded and wore the
pointed hats, the custom of their
ordered service at the shrine.
Each sang the hymns of their
tradition and kept with strict
obedience the rituals of the ages.

Since the Holiday of Hope had come
the Grand Musician was himself the
chief director of the liturgy.
The formality of the great high
adoration was broken by the singing
and dancing crowd that swept
through the Holy Square. The Singer
went before them in a sea of warm
approval till he stood beneath the
towering Shrine of Older Life. It
glittered in the sun and lifted up its
marble proclamation to the world.

An acolyte of lower caste rang a
brazen gong that brought the
roaring crowd to silence and only
then did the Grand Musician rise
to speak.

"What does this uproar mean?" he
asked.

A single voice rose from the sea
of faces. "We have found the long-
awaited Troubadour. He knows the
Ancient Star-Song!"

"Yes! Yes!" cried the throng, "He
knows the Ancient Star-Song—He is
the Troubadour, Son of Earthmaker!"
The mere suggestion of the joyous
prose began the cries of "Halana"
all over again. Once again the
gong restored a silence to the square.
The Grand Musician turned to the Singer.

"Is it true? Are you the Troubadour?
Can you sing the Ancient Star-Song?"

"I am he. I know the song."

"Then sing it now," agreed the Keepers of the Ancient Ways.

The Singer took his lyre and strummed
the strings. The chords fell
outward over all the throng.

The audience grew still. He sang
the very words he first had sung
before his mother. Above him towered
the wall and high upon the bulwark
he saw the framework of a strange machine.
It was the great machine on which
false singers met their death.

He knew then what it meant to sing
a new song.

And then his finger swept the strings
and he began the final verse.

XVII

A finale is not always the best
song but it is always the last.

The Father and his Troubadour
  sat down
Upon the outer rim of space.
  "And here,
My Singer," said Earthmaker,
  "is the crown
Of all my endless skies—the
  green, brown sphere
Of all my hopes." He reached
  and took the round
New planet down, and held it
  to his ear.

"They're crying, Troubadour,"
  he said. "They cry
So hopelessly." He gave the
  little ball
Unto his Son, who also held
  it by
His ear. "Year after weary
  year they all
Keep crying. They seem born to
  weep then die.
Our new man taught them crying
  in the Fall.

"It is a peaceless globe.
  Some are sincere
In desperate desire to see
  her freed
Of her absurdity. But
  war is here.
Men die in conflict, bathed
  in blood and greed."

Then with his nail he scraped
   the atmosphere
And both of them beheld the
   planet bleed.

Earthmaker set earth spinning
   on its way
And said, "Give me your vast
   infinity
My son; I'll wrap it in a bit
   of clay.
Then enter Terra microscop-
   ically
To love the little souls who
   weep away
Their lives." "I will," I said,
   "set Terra free."

And then I fell asleep and all
   awareness fled.
I felt my very being shrinking
   down.
My vastness ebbed away. In dwindling dread,
All size decayed. The universe
   around
Drew back. I woke upon a tiny
   bed
Of straw in one of Terra's
   smaller towns.

And now the great reduction
   has begun:
Earthmaker and his Troubadour
   are one.
And here's the new redeeming
   melody—
The only song that can set
   Terra free.

The Shrine of older days
   must be laid by.
Mankind must see Earthmaker
   left the sky,
And he is with us. They must
   concede that
I am he. They must believe the
   Song or die.

XVIII

Vengeance *(ven'jəns) noun*
1. Eye for eye, tooth for tooth;
a fair, satisfying and rapid
way to a sightless, toothless
world.

Mercy *(mer'sē) noun*
1. The infrequent art of turning
thumbs up on an old antagonist
at the end of one's rapier.

Liar," cried the Keepers of the Ancient Ways, when he had finished with his song. "We've kept this Shrine for many years as our fathers did before us. Earthmaker loves the shrine he gave us. He will meet us here forever."

"No," cried the Singer. "Please believe the Song. Earthmaker never will again meet men within this holy square."

"Liar!" they cried again. "Strike him on the mouth." A bearded monk, who only lately read the liturgy, laid aside his scroll and struck the Singer on the mouth. The blood ran down his chin.

"Listen, men of Terra!" cried the Grand Musician. "He sings a lie. Earthmaker loves the Shrine. He has loved it for a thousand holidays."

The Singer stumbled to his feet and cried above the crowd. "Earthmaker loves neither shrines nor holidays. He loves only men. Life is the Song and not the Shrine." Another Keeper of the Ancient Ways laid aside his incense and his holy book and struck him in the face. He fell once more.

The Madman who had lately sung in joy the great Halana Chorus was

bewildered by this furious turn of
circumstance. When they struck
the Singer the second time he rushed
upon the Keepers of the Ancient Ways.
He attacked them with such fury that
they fell away in fright. Then
suddenly a sentinel struck him from
behind and sent him sprawling in
the dust unconscious. In a moment
they had him clamped securely in the
irons.

"Listen," cried a voice above the
tumult of the moment. The Singer
knew the voice. It was the World
Hater masquerading as a Keeper of
the Ancient Ways. He wore the mask
of those who led in worship at the
Shrine.

"Listen," he said again, "this man
in irons is mad. For years he hung
in chains and quite away from all
that he might hurt until today.
The Singer freed him to attack and
hoped that he might injure the Keepers
of the Ancient Ways.

"Look at him," said the masquerading
World Hater, pointing to the
Singer. "Does he appear a Holy
Singer? Where are his prayer book
and candle? If he had come to
worship, would he not have brought
along a scroll of ancient truths?
If his song is from the Father-
Spirit, why did it not come to us
through the Grand Musician? He
wears no robe, he has no beard
like other holy men. Where is his

pointed hat? He was but a tradesman
in the northern hills. He
never studied music like the Grand
Musician. Is it reasonable to
suppose that God would give a tradesman
a song that he withheld from those
who keep his very Shrine?"

The Grand Musician rose and sang.
Infirmly at the first, but gaining
confidence, he sang the Anthem of
the great Shrine.

"Blessed be Thou, O Earthmaker,
Lover of the ancient days
May we adore the ancient truths,
Walk only on the ancient ways."

Gradually the crowd began to join
the Grand Musician.

"Keep Thy Shrine a sacred place
For practice of Thy timeless lore
Of ancient holy men who taught us
Great traditions we adore."

Finally from the habit of their
worship all the crowd rose up to
sing the songless melody they had
learned from the generations who
had left them with the weariness
of worship.

"Blessed art Thou, O Earthmaker,
Help of ours in ages past,
Keep Thy holy Shrine forever,
Never changing truth Thou hast."

"Long live Earthmaker!" cried a
gray-beard Keeper of the Ancient

Ways. "Long live Earthmaker," he
repeated. "Long live the Shrine of
Older Life."

And all of them called out together,
"Long live Earthmaker. Long live
the Shrine of Older Life."

"What shall we do, O Grand Musician,
with the Liar who hates the Shrine
of Older Life?" cried the Hater
still in masquerade.

"We shall smash his lyre and..."
Before he could name the sentence,
a small bent man made his way to
the steps of the Shrine. It was
the Miller with the injured hand.
"May I speak before you pass the
sentence?" the Miller asked the
Grand Musician.

"You may," he answered back.

"I am a miller. My home is by the
grainfields of the east. Three
years ago my hand was crushed in
an accident at my own mill. This
liar who calls himself the only
Troubadour mocked my crushed
deformity and left me screaming in
the night."

"Had you no pity, Singer,
for this man?" the Grand Musician
asked.

"He had pity enough for himself.
I could have made him whole," the
Singer said.

"How can you call yourself Earthmaker's Son and have no pity?
Earthmaker is merciful and filled
with love." He paced the marble
stones before the crowd. At
length he spoke, "Because you
had no pity your hand shall be
like his."

He thought once more and said,
"And now I pass the sentence. We
shall break his lyre, then we shall
break his hand and set him free.
On the flesh of his forehead we
shall burn the word 'Liar' and he
shall live beneath his sentence
all his life. So shall the sentence
be of anyone who claims to be
Earthmaker's Son and sings a song
which desecrates the Shrine.

"Bring out the block and mallet."

The guards obeyed. They placed the
Singer's hand upon the block and
brought the crushing mallet down.

The Singer winced.

The Miller walked up to the Singer
who gently held his injured hand.

"Would you like pity from me,
Singer?" he said through his teeth.
"Here, Singer, is the only kind of
pity that you know." He spit into
the Singer's face and laughed.

The Madman strained against the
chains and was about to rip them

free. His struggle ended in futility.
He could not look upon the
suffering of the only man who knew
him sane. He cried to see the
spit of hate coursing down the
Singer's face.

"Crush his other hand before you set
him free," cried someone in the
crowd. "Teach him through great pain
that Earthmaker pities injury."

"It's true he must learn how to care,"
the Grand Musician cried. "Place his
other hand upon the block."

Once more the mallet fell and the
splintering of tendons shot burning
agony throughout the Singer's soul.

They laid his lyre upon the block
and smashed it with the mallet
that had fallen twice before.

"Sing for us!" they cried in vengeance.
"Play and sing!" they said.

The Grand Musician turned his head
and sang an ancient hymn while they
spit again upon the Singer and
struck him with their fists.

"You were going to heal the Miller's
hand," cried someone in the crowd.
"Sing healing to your own."

When the Grand Musician finished singing
all the ancient hymn, he turned
back to the Singer who gazed in agony
upon his broken hands. "Bring the

fire and irons and we shall etch the
name upon his face."

They seared the word across his
forehead... L I A R.

The Madman held his shaggy face and
cried into his hands. His sobbing
went unnoticed in the action of
the trial.

"May I now release this false
Troubadour?" the Grand Musician
asked.

"No. He must die upon the wall.
Let him suffer for his lies. Let
him hang where everyone may know
the nature of his ugly melodies of
desecration. Hang him on the
great machine of death."

"Yes! Yes!" they cried in fevered
chanting. "Yes! Yes! thou Great
Musician! Yes! Hang him on the
great machine of death."

XIX

Institutions have a poor safety
record. The guillotines of
orthodoxy keep a clean blade that
is always honed for heresy. And
somewhere near the place where
witches die an unseen sign is
posted whose invisible letters
clearly read:
WE ARE PROUD TO REPORT
0 WORKING DAYS LOST TO
INJURY OR ACCIDENT.
—THE MANAGEMENT

Let us pray.

The sentinels returned the Madman
to the grove. He followed them
without a struggle. He walked
along in the stupefaction of his
disbelief. In his former
madness he would have crushed the
wardens in the foment of his rage.
He could scarcely understand that
in a single day he had been
granted both a new mind and an
injured heart.

The day's proceedings had been too
much for him. Every time he closed
his eyes, he saw the mallet of the
executioner again: The splintering
of tendons, the wincing of the Singer,
the facial blows the priest had
given him: all these made his mind
a horror chamber.

Somewhere in his reverie of agony
they reached the wall. The attendants
locked him in the irons, while
he stared vacantly away. They
brought him bread and water, which
he never saw.

He only wept. A tremor shook his
giant frame.

The darkness came. The Madman cried.
While somewhere higher on the wall
the Singer died.

It was good the Madman could not
behold his suffering. He could

not have borne it. A trinity of
other lovers came, all three
absorbed in one great hurt.
The little girl sat down between
the older women.

"I am his mother," said the oldest.
"I am the demonstration of his
power," said the little girl.
"I am only a friend," said the
other woman.

"I gave him life," said his mother.
"I gave him twisted feet," said the
little girl.
"I gave him shame," said the friend.

"He taught me obedience to the Father-
Spirit," said the mother.
"He taught me running."
"He taught me love."

They sat beneath the great machine of
death. It was a trebled pietà of
stone and still it wept.

"I feel very old today," said the
mother as she placed her arm around
the shoulder of the little girl.

"I feel as though I soon must
watch the Father-Spirit die." The
girl sobbed into the bosom of the
Singer's mother.

The Friendship Seller was a
world away. She said, "I am
ashamed of being human. It
is the very shame I felt the first
time that I..." She could not

bring herself to tell her ugly
fall before the grieving child.
"The moment that I saw the Keeper
of the Ancient Ways who was chief
accuser, I knew he bore some vague
familiarity. He was no priest..."

"I know," the older woman said.

"He was the piper who taught me a
song of death and called it love,"
the Friendship Seller said.

"I knew him too," said the little
girl. "He used to pass me where
I begged, and look upon my twisted
legs and laugh. I used to feel so
bad when he would look and smirk
in satisfaction. And every time he
passed he left me crying."

They ceased their talking and
looked up at the wall. The great
machine hung heaviness into
their souls, the giant timbers
creaked in the ordeal they were
asked to undergo. The women shuddered
when they viewed the suffering
form that lay among the cables
and the gears.

Grief owned the day.

In turn the three stood up and
stared upon the dying Singer, high
and lifted up.

"My joy, my health," said the little
girl.

"My life," said the Friendship Seller.

The night stood dumb. The burdened
mother wept. "The Ancient Star-
Song lost. The World Hater won.
I wish I might have died instead
of you, my son, my son, my son."

XX

A child who cries at the
coffin of his father is
only mature when he has
lived long enough to cry
at the coffin of his son.

Never was a boy crucified,
but that the weeping Father
always found the nail-prints
in his own hands.

The dying went slowly. The great
timbers were weathered by
the grimness of their task. A
single, great gear pivoted upon
an axis, that culminated in a
windlass upon which wound a cable.
Below in an ever tightening arc an
armature was turning. A group of
smaller cams and gears seemed each
to play their part in keeping
tension on the heavy ropes.

The beams and cables ended where a
set of chains fastened their steel
bands to the hands and feet of the
Singer. Each time the great windlass
moved a fraction of an inch,
the tension grew upon the ropes and
left the Singer caught in agony that
grew increasingly unbearable.

Suspended from a rough-hewn crane
there hung a hopper. And everyone
who lived within the ancient city
filed silently along the wall and
dropped a stone within the great
receptacle. The growing weight
increased the stress. The lines groaned
upon the metal bands.

The Keepers of the Ancient Ways
began the execution by laying on
the stones of offense first. It
was their holy stones of accusation that set the great machine
in motion. In fidelity to the
truth, they bowed their knees and

looked to heaven and chanted in
the file of death.

Oh God of ancient days,
Thou Keeper of the Ancient Ways,
Our fathers' God, we praise!

Over and over ran the litany of
death. The weight of accusation
grew with each successive stone.

The Singer seemed small among
the heavy beams of wood. The gray
of the day settled close around the
spiraled towers and by the afternoon,
the fog removed the upper walls from
sight. Still it settled downward.
At last the great machine itself was
shrouded by the mist that came to
cool the fever in the dying Singer.

When the fog had made the city one
great livid criminal, the Singer
looked through glazed eyes and
saw his foe, sitting on an old
and rotten beam. He leered
above the stretched and dying man
before him.

"You give me joy and music you
will never hear, Singer. Groan
for me. Scream the fire that
fills your soul. Spew the venom
of your grudge upon the city.
Never have I known the triumph
of my hate till now."

He rose and walked across the beam
and stepped upon a cable. The added
strain drew the manacles into the

wrists of the dying Singer.

"Check-mate, Singer!" He howled into
the mist and the shrieking of his
laughter was absorbed into the opaque
air.

The Singer felt the agony of dying,
the multiplied pain of a hundred thousand
men all dying at one time.

With an agility of delight the Hater
danced his way around the armature
and strutted on the ropes. He looked
into the fog again and shouted,
"Your move, Earthmaker!"

The great, gray, unseen walls grabbed
the mockery and flung their sonic
echoes from stone to stone. And while
the reverberations rang throughout the
Great Walled City, the Hater in sadistic
gaiety ran out upon the ropes,
swung around a beam and threw
his words outward into the sick sky.

"I have you crying, Earthmaker. You
can never glory in your universal
riches, for I have made you poor. And
there is none to pity you. Everyone
you made has retired to eat and drink
away their absurd holiday, and when
they wake up in the morning their great
machine will have done its work.
You lie at man's caprice and wait for
him to break your heart... Earthmaker
is crying at the mercy of his earth.

"You started crying when they broke
his hands. Can it be that the agony

which plunges you in grief can wash
my soul with joy?

"Look how he dies. Cry, Creator, Cry!
This is my day to stand upon the
breast of God and claim my victory
over love. You lost the gamble. In
but an hour your lover will be pulp
upon the gallows. Did you tell him
when his fingers formed the world,
that he would die on Terra, groaning
with his hands crushed and whimpering
in my great machine?"

He laughed and turned to look again
upon the Troubadour.

"Now, who will sing the Father-Spirit's
Song?" he asked the dying man.

The Singer seemed to rally in his
suffering. From somewhere far beyond
himself he drew a final surge
of strength and sang the final verse
again.

"And now the great reduction has begun:
Earthmaker and his Troubadour are one."

He sang. And then his lips fell silently
apart and his head slumped forward
on his chest.

The Father-Spirit wept.

The fog swirled in bleak and utter
numbness.

Existence raved.

The stones bled.

The Shrine of Older Life collapsed
in rubble.

And Terra shuddered in her awful crime.

XXI

Decision is the key to destiny.

"God, can you be merciful and send
me off to hell and lock me in
forever?"

"No, Pilgrim, I will not send you
there, but if you chose to go
there, I could never lock you out."

The Hater cringed to hear the
sound he feared above all else.
The doorway of the worlds stood
open. He felt the giant key
that dangled from his belt. He
wished to gloat a little longer
in his victory but left the
silent gallows where the Singer
was as dead as the rotting beams
of the machine.

He reached the threshold of
eternity and found the doorway
of the worlds not only open but
clearly ripped away. He strained
to hear the everlasting wail, the
eternal dying which he loved.
All was silent. Then he heard
the Song.

"No," he cried. "Give me back
the door and key for this is my
domain." He felt again and found
the great key at his waist had
disappeared.

"Where is the key? Where is the
key?" the Hater cried. But all
the while the Hater knew. Each
man on Terra had a key. And
never could they come into the
Canyon of the Damned unless they
chose to do it. To live there,
men would have to reject the Song.
It was a song that only four
on Terra knew, but it would grow until
the world could sing it.

"Earthmaker, this day was not the
victory I had thought," the World Hater
cried. "We both have lost. You
have lost your Son and I have
lost my kingdom."

It was a hollow loss. Full well
the Hater knew the Canyon of the
Damned would never be as large as
he had hoped.

He steeled himself for the battle
out ahead.

He would have to fight the Song.
He would fight with every
weapon in his arsenal of hate.

But he knew that he would lose.
And he knew that when the course of
time was done, the door would be
put back upon the Canyon of the
Damned, and he would be locked
in with all the discord of the
universe. And he would suffer
with all of those he had taught
to hate the Song or consciously
ignore it.

And he himself would be a prisoner
of the hate he spread on Terra.
And when the doorway of the worlds
was locked the final time, he
himself would be inside the Canyon of
the Damned.

And only God would have the key.

XXII

WHEN GOD LOSES HIS BELOVED
habeas corpus is a weak and futile
law. But Earthlings never seem to
learn that it is futile to dredge
the graveyards for messiahs. No
matter how intently you may man
the cables, the grappling hooks
will always come up empty.

In the morning, the wreckage of the
great machine lay in splintered
beams beneath the wall. It had
fallen in the night. The great iron
pinions that held it to the ancient
stones had given way.

The whole affair had been so wrapped
in mist that none had seen its fall.
But all had heard the roar and crash
of its collapse.

The city had not slept. A common
guilt had kept them thinking of the
man who died above them and the
holiday that they had passed in emptiness.
And when they had tried to sleep, the
image of the Singer etched itself upon
the darkness of the night. They felt
unspoken shame in merely being sons
and grandsons of the masons and
carpenters who had made the great machine
in centuries long gone.

When Terra shuddered in the night, the
old machine had torn itself away and
splintered in a single heap of rotted
wood and rusted iron. And many in the
peaceless night remarked that it was
odd the Singer and the old machine
should die the self-same moment.

Shortly after daybreak the wreckage
lay behind a civil barricade
and a crew of laborers was sent
to clear the chaos from the
streets. A group of men lifted

the heavy beams. Ox-drawn sledges took
them well beyond the city gates.

Each workman feared that he
might be the one to come upon
the mangled body of the Singer who
now lay buried in the last
remains of the machine. The heavy
drayage of debris lasted into early
afternoon.

A workman finally spied the giant
tension cable that drew the heavy
chains. He feared to see the
mutilation he would find beneath
the tangled cables and the ropes.

But when he had pulled the final
chains away, the manacles were empty.
And where the Singer should have
been there lay only a key—a great
key forged from a metal never mined
on earth. When the workman stooped
to pick it up he found that it was
broken. It was clear that whatever door
it might have fit would never see its
use again. That nameless door
would remain forever locked or open. For
a moment the workman wondered which.
"Open," he thought. "Yes, definitely
open."

He pondered the great key. Was it of any
consequence? Should he report it to the
Grand Musician? He finally threw
the broken key into a passing
ox-cart filled with wreckage. He
shrugged his shoulders and set out to
find the overseer.

At length he found the foreman sent to direct the clean-up operation at the wall. "Tell the Grand Musician," he said, "there is no body in the wreckage and the manacles are empty."

XXIII

"What would you like to be when you grow up, little girl?"

"Alive."

The child lay wide awake and
filled with fear. Something dreadful
in the dying of her friend left
her trembling in the cold. To be
an orphan in a world that took
so little thought of homeless
children was tenuous enough. But a
greater dread stalked her smaller
world. The Singer was no more,
and she felt again the way she
had before he came and found her
begging by the roadside.

"Please keep me well," she prayed.
"Father-Spirit, keep me as the
Singer left me." She felt her
little legs to be quite sure they
had not withered in the night.
"Now that he is gone, please,
Father-Spirit," she pled into
the darkness, "must I become
an invalid again?"

In every shadow of the night she saw
the lurking image of the World Hater.
She remembered how he leered at her
and smirked to see her in the
roadside dust. "Oh, Father, it is
better that I had not received
the gift of motion than to have
gained and lost it. I never
can go back again to crawling
in the streets," she sobbed. "Please
do not make me crawl again and
beg. Oh, Father, please..."

The first faint coloring of dawn

found her lying in fatigue,
still begging for her legs which
had not suffered any loss for
all her worry. But her agony and doubt
had caused her view of things
to grow narrow in the night.
Even the first pale light of day
did not reveal the world that
really was.

She felt someone beside her on the
simple mat that was her bed.

"You worried about your legs for
nothing," said a voice.

She sat upright in her fear.
In but a moment she was on
her feet and seemed about to run.
Then she looked at him more fully.
Her heart was pumping. "Can it be?"
And she concluded in her madness,
"It is!" She threw herself into
the Singer's arms with such a strong
embrace it all but knocked him over.
"You're alive—alive." She closed
her eyes and opened them to be sure
that blinking would not erase her joy.
"Oh, Singer—I was so afraid. I
thought my legs would be as..."

"Yours are better far than mine this
morning," he said.

His hands and feet were barely recog-
nizable. She who had cried for
her own legs was overcome by real
concern for his.

"You healed mine!" she said. "Heal

your own. Please, Singer, make them
well."

"They are well. There is no pain
now."

"But they are scarred and
wounded. How can they be well?"

"Earthmaker leaves the scars, for
they preserve the memory of pain.
He will leave my hands this way
so men will not forget what it can
cost to be a singer in a theater
of hate."

"But the word . . . the word they
wrote upon your face is gone."

The Singer reached up to his forehead
where the searing iron had left
the accusation of the council.
The word was gone indeed.

"It is," he said, "because Earthmaker
cannot bear a lie. He could not let
me wear the word for He is Truth.
He knows no contradiction in himself.
So learn this, my little friend, no
man may burn a label into flesh and
make it stay when heaven disagrees."

"But did the Father-Spirit agree
with all the other things they did
to your hands and feet?"

"He wished they had not done it . . .
But, yes . . . he did agree that without
these wounds Terra could not know
how much he loved her. You will find,

my child, that love rarely ever
reaches out to save except it does
it with a broken hand."

She seemed to understand, and because
he loved her childish eyes so much
he made her ready for the future.

"Do you love me, child?" he asked.

"With all my heart," she answered.

"And would you give me anything I
asked of you?" he said.

"Anything!" she answered.

"It may be hard to give me all I
ask. Not long ago, in the name of
love, I gave you legs. Yesterday
that very love demanded mine. But
the Song is all that matters. It
may be you will have to sing it
where the crowd will shout you
down and demand your legs or life.
But it would be far better to give
them both than to surrender up the
music in your soul. Some will
hate you for the song you love.
They will seek to stop your singing.
But no matter how they treat you,
remember that I suffered everything
before you. And if they should
brand you with a name across
your face..."

"It cannot stay, if heaven disagrees,"
she finished up his statement.

He had stretched her small philosophy.

But he knew that she was growing
in her understanding of the Song.

"Let us stop our talking and say that
for right now it is enough to be a
little girl with two good legs and to
know the sun is shining. Let's go
out into the fields together. Are you
afraid to hold my wounded hand?"
he asked. "It is so ugly."

"It is so beautiful," she disagreed.
He held out his gentle
hand. She placed her little hand
in his and was surprised to
find that when his hand had
closed around her own he had a
healthy grip. "Your hand is firm
and strong. God did not leave it
broken long," she said.

"He never does," he answered.

Hand in hand they walked.
The sunlight brought the brightest
day the world had ever known.
She held his hand as if to
never let him go. She skipped at the
base of her shadow and danced the
way she had the very day they met.

"I'm sorry I had doubts about my
legs," she said, then asked, "Where
are we going?"

"To a man who has some doubts about
his mind."

XXIV

Every constellation is but a
gathering of distant suns. It is
mere perspective that makes
Betelgeuse a star. Seen close
enough she is a raging fire.
A sphere of flaming hydrogen, if it
be nearer, will dominate the sky
and blot out all the lesser lights.
And such a fire will say again,
"Earthmaker has a living Son."

The sunlight came much later to
the wall than it did to city
streets. Two women hurried
through the purple and the silver
light of dawn toward the grove
where they knew the sentinels
had led the Madman. The trees in
darkness were menacing and thick.
They kept upon the path until
the dark and ancient wall towered
over them.

"How can we find him in this gloom?"
the younger woman asked.

Before the question could be answered,
they heard the clanking of his chains.
The terrifying sound made them
fear him all the more.

"Madman... please... we are your
friends... I am the Singer's mother...
I saw you try to save him at the
trial..." Her words fell out in
unconnected phrases.

When their eyes had grown accustomed
to the light, they found him crumpled like a titan child against
the wall. No more a threat.

"Go away," he said, moving very
little.

"Please, Madman... we are your friends.
I really am the mother of the man
you would have saved."

The other woman said nothing as the
two of them continued. The Madman
said in his despair, "No one could
save him... the World Hater won.
He spent the night in laughter
at the gallows."

"I loved my son," the mother said,
"and I must thank you for loving him
as I."

"Yes, I loved him. For one brief day,
my mind was well... so short a time. I
knew meaning and reason. But now he's
dead."

"And I with him," she said.

"Today the Hater will be back,"
the Madman said, "with his absurd
pipe. He will play and play until
he leaves me foaming in insanity
again. I'll writhe and wallow
to his joy and die in
hopeless chains."

"We all have chains," at length
the silent woman joined in.
"I too may go back to chains I
thought I'd left for good. When
I try to sing the Ancient Star-Song
the verses are disjointed and
apart."

"I cannot tell how long my mind
will stay when hate returns today,"
sighed the Madman.

The sunlight broke and came at once
above the wall and ran in golden

streams along the blackened stones.
It set the grove aglow with bronze
earth and green wax leaves. The
gray was swallowed up in color and
an oriole sang deep-throated joy.

The three sat in the instant
morning that had baptized them
with suddenness and left them
studying the pathway through the
grove. At the far end, they saw
a little girl walking hand in hand
with a tall man.

On a little knoll of ground just
outside the grove, the stranger
stopped and released the child
and threw his arms into the air
and wrapped a melody in sunlight
and threw the triumph of the morning
against the grove and wall.

"In the beginning was the song of
love," he sang.

The two women were on their feet
within the instant and running
toward the thrilling song that came
with day.

The Madman stood and strained
against his chains. He could not
move, although he threw his massive
weight against the iron that held
him from the Singer. The steel
cut his wrists but did not break.
Then at the zenith of his struggle
he remembered all at once the
principle of reason. He let back
on the chains till they were slack.

"Once more, Lord," he called out
through the trees. "Once more."

Again the Singer lifted up his
bearded head and sang, "In the
beginning was the song of love..."
And through the trees the Madman's
strong sound voice sang back, "And
here's the new redeeming melody, the
only song that can set Terra free."

The chains unlocked themselves and
fell away. The Madman left the dark
and hurried into day.

Like autumn leaves triumph swirled upward
into sky. The song came on forever.

And distant quasars hurrying in
space marveled that the dull and joyless world had finally come of age.

Thus Terra joined the universe who
knew the song so long before, when
the parent stars themselves were
tracked by wounded feet. And for
a thousand years the music never
ceased. It ricocheted through
canyons and hung in promise over
all of Terra's seas.

And those who know the Ancient Star-
Song watch with singing for the
sign of footprints in the galaxies
through which the little planet
rides in routine cycles of despair.
But Joy seldom sleeps for long.
And someday in a lonely moment mankind will shake an unfamiliar hand
and find it wounded.

THE
SONG

1

In the middle of the faithless
sky there hangs a small, dark
world that once was green and
blue.

Some say it killed itself by
stabbing all its lovely lands
with deep atomic wounds.
Some say it took an overdose
of hate.

When words are rare as gems,
then sentences are mined at
great expense. In such a time
the tiny planet Terra swung
its mindless orbits in constant
hunger for a word that would
not come. Silence stalked the
universe and Earthmaker would
not speak. There was little
that his love could say to
a vicious world so fond of
tearing holes in his beloved.

It was agreed by common guilt
that spirit had turned its back
on matter. Earthmaker had set
his face away from the place of
execution and was staring outward
toward glittering and unspoiled
star-fields. For Terra was a field
of tombs—a universal junkyard where
his creatures quarreled for refuse
and waged great wars over who
should own the wreckage of their times.

Messiahs were abundant, but all
of them were egotists who hawked
joy-plated creeds through their
fading empires.

The men of Terra made a dull
discovery in the tepid days
that closed upon the Singer's
disappearance: When Earthmaker
will not speak to men, they have
nothing of importance to say to
each other.

II

There is but one good illustration
of SPIRIT—WIND!
Everything else is too visible.

When Spirit comes to flesh
gales rage and zephyrs scream.
When he withdraws, air
stagnates and insects
build webs in the rotors
of the silent mills.

The Madman spoke only words
that would not wait—
the small and mindless things
it took to keep life at a
distance great enough
to breathe.

The thick, hot air clotted commerce
and forced all men to wade its deadness.
The desert leered at villagers
and waited with the condors for
life to change to carrion.

The Madman took his turn in the line
at the village well. Like all the
rest he held a bucket which he hoped
to fill. Everyone in line still nursed
the fear that the ancient well
would fail. When it did, the
town would die. Each man hoped for
rain and begged the question:
"When comes the wind?"

The Madman felt the final hint of
moving air the day the Singer left—
the day the sun moved closer and
the breezes stopped. Half-truths
had festered in the lifeless air,
for most believed The Lie which
taught the Singer had died that
shrouded night the timbers
tumbled to the ground.

Rumors raged. Doubt was universal
for the scholars agreed that no
one could live through the cursed

ordeal of the machine, much less
its fall from ancient battlements.

There were some who said the
drought that fell upon the world
was the vengeance of the mountain
gods angered at the cruelty of
"holy men" who murdered only when
they wore the sacred garb of priests.
Some said it thundered twice each
day at the precise and awful moment
that they broke his hands. Yet
it never thundered on the plains
—only in the highlands.

The sun kept shorter nights and
walked a slower arch across the
cloudless skies. The dry earth
cracked its wrinkled, powdered
crust. The well rope grew dry
further down its braided coil,
and the water-bearers fell at
midday under shaded eaves.

III

What do you have, young prophet
    bold?
Some new, wide dream of scope?
Written by fire in the snowy cold
On silver plates of hope?

I found him under a tree grown old
And hanged with a doctrine rope.
Some said he thought the tree was
    young.

On the first day of the month of
Krios an old woman came from the
mountains and, bent above her gnarled
stick, she made her way from door
to door. She sang in feeble syllables
the song the Grand Musician once
had sung before official executioners.
She bore a weathered scroll beneath
her tattered sleeve and sang her
tuneless, toneless, tasteless dirge.

She was deaf but quite devoted,
committed to the creed she sang
aloud but had not heard in years.

They asked her if the wind blew in
the mountains. She could not hear,
but the musty odor made it clear
no breeze had blown on her.
Her scroll had not been ruffled by
the mountain wind nor moistened by
the rain. The dust upon the ragged
roll had not been stirred to rise
or settle back again.

While she stood in line before the well,
she died. She did not fall. She only
stared in death as she had stared in life.
And no one seemed to know the
instant of her passing. The
village sexton found her hard
to bury. Her passing seemed a
little matter. No one mourned.

The first of Krios passed.
And on the second of the month
the Madman prayed again,

"Earthmaker, Father of the Singer,
send us now the ancient wind
of promise." He knew the wind
he craved would bring the rain.

He knew that Terra's lover was also
the Keeper of the Winds. And while
he could not know the exact galactic
place, he knew the great Father-Spirit
sat starward in the breeding place
of suns. His light-blazed dais
was founded on the filaments of
constellations never seen on Terra.
And there where all the universal
light converged, and slightly to the
right, stood erect the object of all
universal joy—the Singer, who waited
for Earthmaker to send him back again
into the world that they both loved.

As the planet measured time, the
time was near. The third of Krios
stood just a dawn away. And when
it came, the Court of Ages Gone
would wait in rapt salute until
the Singer folded all his singing
soul into the gracious wind. And
then the raging gales would leave the
splendor of foreverness and break
in hurricanes of love upon the
thirsty world.

The Madman rose from prayer and
walked at noon toward the well.
In the burning way he met a man
who bore a shovel and a scroll.

"Good day, Sexton!" he called.
"You feel compelled to bury
scrolls?"

"No, Madman, I took it from the old
woman who died in the water line,"
the sexton answered. "Old women
should be buried, but never books.
Do you read?"

"I read," the Madman said.

"Then here," said the sexton as he
handed him the woman's one possession.

The Madman took the roll and stared
in fascination at its crinkled skin.
"The book is old," he thought.
"She must have started writing
it when she was very young."

He waited for his measure of water
and then he left the well. He entered his barren room and waited
in the shuttered silence for the
dusk. He ate a crust of bread and
drank a little water. The water,
like the earth, was dead. Nothing
sparkled on the tongue. When darkness
came, he lit an oil wick and broke
the heavy seal upon the scroll. It
opened to the very place of promise
and the ancient words stared up at him.

"The writer was the woman, prior to her
blindness," he said into the gloom.

She had indeed written all the scroll,
this strange old Amazon, whose stories
coursed with dragons and winged
creatures she had seen. Sometimes she
wrote of armies, their conflict set
in blood. And then again she told of
shepherds singing songs and maidens deep

in love with unremembered sheiks.
Sometimes she wrote the mindless,
droning genealogies of her glorious
heritage. Law was there.
Love was there.
Life, justice, death.

The lamp burned low before his eyes
fell on the Song of Promise. The
text came up in joy and hung about
him, robed in the simple glory of
its years:

"O clap your hands
    you dying heads of state!
His love will come to cleanse
    the practiced hate
    of fallen Terra.
Joy will come again
    to fill the deserts,
    level mountain chains.

Earthmaker is in love
    with loveless men.
The God of Storms and Keeper
    of the Winds will come.
The Father-Spirit's only Troubadour
    reserves the heavy gales
    behind the door of Life.
Cry out remorse for hate and sin.
Life comes for all,
    astride the Singing Wind."

IV

An old woman buried three sons.
At the funeral of the first she was
a cynic.
At the funeral of the second she
called herself a seeker.
At the third... a weeping
believer.

By evening, those who waited for
the wind did so in despair. Gaunt
and face to face with death, they knew
the dying was not hard; the burning
journey into death would be. The
children whimpered for the bread
and water that soon would cease.

Some blamed the Father-Spirit.
Some did not.

The yellow earth like dry rot stole
the hope of day and caused old men
to pull their leprous rags about
their ochre faces and spit into the
jaundiced sky and curse Earthmaker.

A mother of twins stood waiting
while the dry well rope uncoiled
from around the crank. She heard
the clatter of the empty bucket
on the rocks below . . . The
rope began to wrap itself around
the windlass once again. When it
reached the top, the bucket and
the rope were dry. So were the men
of Terra, for the time they feared
had come.

In hopeless hope the rope was once
more lowered in the well. Again
the bucket came up dry. Anger
swelled and a temper-ridden man
strode to the well and grabbed
the sexton by his coat. He raised
his voice indignantly and cursed
the sexton for the failure of the well.

His babbled threats were sounds
that never would make words.
The sexton, paralyzed, struggled hard
to understand; he tried to speak
to his assailant, but his earnestness
was also lost in strange new sounds.
Another man came from the crowd to
arbitrate and though his sounds were
syllables of peace he too could form
no words.

Fear came upon the city. Words,
like water, ceased to be. Paragraphs
of gibberish proceeded, but not communication. Wails without words rose
from the yellow dust.

Anxiety closed in with night.
A wordless mass hysteria became the
common dread that each one knew but
none could speak. And when words
die, the little fears become the
terrors of the night. They knew
that death would come and when
it did all men would die without
a cry of hope or sensible despair.
No final statements and no eulogies
—no reaching out for touch. Life
would die together—all, at once,
yet separately. And none could
even say "Good-bye!"

Terra kills, but Terra will not die.
Heartless Terra will not even
Let her children cry.
Terra is a spinning vault,
A mass of dusty graves,
The tombyard of her dreamers,
The mausoleum of her brave.

Terra has just one stone
To mark her great insanity:
Across her continents it reads:
"HERE LIES HUMANITY!"

Death is a crone

who grins only when the pulse

is weak, and smiles only in

full when breathing stops.

She grasps her dying

globe and smiles—

a grim madonna gloating on her

sickly child.

As the wail rose in the streets,
Sarkon, the World Hater, smiled at
a triumph which he knew would be
short-lived. He braced himself
for what he saw ahead. He had
decided to become the herald of
the mountain gods, though all the
mountain gods were dead.

He hated Terra as he always had.
He gloated on her exile, pleased
that her disease was terminal.
Like other aging planets, she would
die. But well he knew her time of
dying was not yet. She would recover
from the current illness in her streets
and die when men were more intelligent—
less wise.

In the meantime he would try
to draw men from Earthmaker. He
would need a trick or two and
for his purposes non-existent gods
would do.

Sarkon liked the mountain gods
for they were made in man's own
image. He knew what mortals never
seemed to learn: The more the gods
become like men, the easier it is
for men to believe the gods. When
both have only human appetites, then
rogues may worship rogues.

Meanwhile he enjoyed seeing
Terra at the point of death. He
smiled because her desperation was

intense. He made his way through
the streets to the quarters of a
man he had met a thousand times
before, but when he reached the
Madman's door, a sheet of fire
blocked his way.

Inside, the great Earthmaker drew
a soft embrace around his lonely
child, who sought to pray the sickness from the streets.

"It is good to be your child,
Earthmaker," the Madman said aloud.

"It is good to own you," said
the darkness with impressive
silence. "Madman, you are sane—
more sane than any dweller on this
orb. You may no longer wear a
name that lies. From now you will
be Anthem, for you will be the
Herald of the Anointing. The
power of Earthmaker will be yours,
to bear the Singer and his Song
before the kings of Terra."

Then Anthem fondled his new name,
and turned it over in his heart.
Tomorrow he would take his name
and enter a new age. Tomorrow he
would come and bring with him the
promised Age of Gold. His name was
quite as eloquent as that great flame
that kept his gate. The fiery wall
left Sarkon a vagabond to walk alone
in hate.

VI

It takes a breeze
to make a banner speak.

The third of Krios wrapped itself
in gray. The sun was merciful and
never rose. The morning brought a
breeze that stiffened to a gale. The
welcome smell of sweet young rain
became a furied hint of promises the
heavens shortly kept. Rain drenched
the earth in torrents of the love
that great Father-Spirit now scattered
in the dust.

So Terra came alive and people ran
into the streets to feel the water
and the wind. None were ashamed
to see themselves soaked in driving,
blinding rain.

It was the changing of the age—
the great fulfillment of the ancient
vow the woman wrote down in her
scroll. And as the rain streamed
down his face, Anthem also praised
Earthmaker that his Beloved had come
back. He stood and shouted out
above the crowd:
"Earthmaker rides the Wind.
The Singer has returned . . ."

Silence roared.
Sound ripped through density.
Communication coursed again
through human isolation. And
Anthem spoke—no longer gibberish—
but words and sentences, and all his
words were understood.

"How is it," cried the crowd,
"that we now hear with understanding
and the gift of words is given?"

When Anthem raised his hand and
called the wild excitement to a
calm, the wind made way for words.
His Wind Song then began.

"The Eagle has returned.
    The shattered sky
Has fallen back. And Terra's
    victory
Is sure. The Singer whom we
    caused to die
Has come to slay time
    with infinity.

The Father-Spirit and his
    Troubadour
Have brought the Great Invader
    and his Age
Of Gold. For they were old
    when nature tore
Away the vacuum at its heart.
    Love raged.

And then the trebled Spirit
    mystery
Was one. Yet love begun
    in open space
Would swell in joy till
    one was three—
His factor of infinity
    in grace.

And never shall his Terra
    understand
This cosmic riddle born
    ahead of men;

How Spirit can become
   a sinewed hand
And then a cosmic Spirit
   once again.

Never was it one but
   always three.
Never was it three but
   always one.
Claiming boldly it would
   always be—
Yet crying out it never
   had begun.

Let men embrace the rain.
   Come, Wind, blow free
And stir the warm sweet breeze!
   Dream, dreamless men!
Our empty youth come filled
   with prophecy.
Our grunts now Spirit-washed
   are words again.

The Great Invader breathes upon you
   as a man
Of Holy Fire, from that far land
   where all
Horizons meet. He knocks
   with wounded hands
Upon the soul. And penetrates
   the wall

Of your resistance to Earthmaker's
   love.
The Spirit of the Singer
   comes to sing
An inner melody.
   To fill above
Our brim of joy his own
   abundant being.

Weep, Terra! For yours is
   the ugly crime
That killed the Song and struck
   Earthmaker dumb.
You stabbed eternal life
   with dismal time
And murdered him who was and
   is to come.

O men of Terra! Ours is
   the shame,
Of standing heavy-footed
   on his name.
Beside the star-blazed dais
   there he stands.
We clawed the face of love then
   broke his hands.

Cry out! O men, cry out! The blood
   we spilt
Has left us refugees from love.
   And sin
Has left us in a wilderness
   of guilt.
Trust in the joy that swims
   Invader's Wind."

And then the rain drew back, and eerie
light converged upon the rain-soaked
streets. A column of brightness
gathered itself from the gleam of
cobblestones and fled in a fiery instant
into the sky.

And at the top a mystic beam of majesty
tumbled down in music. A chord then
turned to thunder that shook the earth.
Earthmaker so blazed in radiance
that men cried out in fear and love
at once.

The dazzling hurricane of light
fell full on Terra's shame
and a fiery brilliant radiance
proclaimed his mighty name—
Invader.

VII

Where do the old gods live?
  In temples tended by old, old men.
And the young gods?
  In young men who dream
  of building temples so that they
  will have something to tend when
  they are old, old men.
It is better to believe than dream.
For dreams grow old and so do
  dreamers.
Dreamers die but not believers.

An old man lifted up his face and
wept before the transfixed crowd.
He called out through his tears,
"What must I do to be unchained?"

And Anthem answered, "Admit your
emptiness. Open to the Wind.
Receive the Stigmon of the Singer."

"I will. Come in, Invader," he
cried into the swirling radiance.
He held his leathered face in
wrinkled hands, and when he
took his hands away, he wore a
strange new countenance of light.

Anthem reached down and scooped
a handful of moist earth.
"Do you believe the Singer is
alive and that he is Earthmaker's Son?"

"Yes," cried the old man in a husky
voice, choked by the fullness of
his joy.

"Then," said Anthem, "receive the
Stigmon." He traced upon the old man's
face the Singer's Sign with earth
and spoke:
"It is only out of Terra's shame
That men of Terra wear the name
Of Singer,
Prince of Planets,
Troubadour of Life."

And then he placed a small amount
of the remaining soil in the old

man's hand, as he breathed the last
lines of the Stigmon:
"Remember as your hand is stained
That his was crushed and torn by pain
That men of Terra fully know
There is no depth he would not go
To Love.
Earthmaker, Singer and Invader be
The substance of infinity."

The old man suddenly found himself in a
sea of thirsty faces crying out to the
Invader to enter them in the storm of
light that now enveloped all.

Hundreds were invaded and the Singer
added to this number all who were unchained and had received the Stigmon.
Their foreheads were smudged with
the Singer's Sign and their hands bore
the symbol of his wounds.

The day was long and lovely and
substance slept with a thousand hearts
by fall of night. It was the dawning
of the Age of the Invader.

VIII

The fable reminds us:

A witch may beguile us with apples!

Beware old women selling green fruit.
Their sales deceive.

Who spares a witch may but
  a serpent save.
A dying dragon digs a witch's grave.
We seldom trust the fairy tales
Until we gasp in claws and scales.

Anthem slept a lovely sleep that
would have lasted through the night
except the fire before his gate
was gone. So in the center of
the night he was awakened by the
rapping of an old familiar hand
outside his room. He lit the lamp
and opened up the door. His faint
light fell into the night before
the fingers of the dark pinched
out the amber fire.

Seeing no one, he closed the door, then
bolted it in fear. And sitting on his
bed he called into the dark, "Hater,
give back my flame." The darkness
would not answer him, till in a firmer
voice he almost shouted,
"I now command you in the
Singer's name and the name of his
machine of death, give back my light
and then give substance to yourself."

Instantly the lamp relit itself.
Its light fell out upon a handsome
youth.

"Are you unchained?" the young man
asked.

"Yes," Anthem said. He tried to
match the fairness of the youth
with what he thought that he would
see. "I want all the light you took
from me, World Hater!"

The flame burned brighter still.

"Yes, I'm unchained—invaded, too."
Then Anthem spoke in boldness, "I
know you are the World Hater in
disguise. And I no longer fear the
pipe you play that once drove me
insane."

"I gave my pipe away, Madman..."
His voice trailed off in huskiness.

"My name is not Madman, it is
Anthem. The Father-Spirit says I
am too sane to wear the name you
gave me, Hater."

"Please... do not call me World
Hater now—my name is Sarkon."

"You do still hate the world?"

The boy then smirked. The tendons
rippled in his ivory neck. He drew
a slur across his heavy lips. "Of
course I hate. But Terra will not
know. Every one will see Sarkon
a lover whose affection is much
stronger than the love of..."
His mouth still moved but would not
frame the word.

"You cannot say 'The Singer' can you?
Your hate has no coordination
for such a lovely name."

"Yes," the youth went on, "I, Sarkon,
will pose as Terra's lover, try to
pry her from her track and roll her
into some galactic hole filled with
stellar putrefaction. I am committed
to her last destruction. I have

infected every corner with the desire
for power and greed, as you will see.
I have smeared the continents with
lust for blood not even your Invader
can swab clean."

"A thousand were unchained today,"
said Anthem.

"But millions still are mine and
hate the myth you love."

"It isn't myth, Hater!"

"I've told you that my name is
Sarkon now. Do you notice
any newer facets to my form,
Anthem?"

"You're taller somehow. Studied,
handsome, muscular. Your hair looks
like a sculptured head I once saw in
a pagan shrine. You look much like
a mountain god."

Sarkon was delighted. "I am—
fresh from a temple men can see.
Yes, I am man as he was meant to
be—ideal humanity—managerial and
strong, empirical and wise
with answers that are more visible
than yours. And I know science
too. Come talk with me about
creation and you will be embarrassed
by my questions."

Anthem grew angry. "I thought
you said you would have answers
from your sciences and now you
talk of questions."

"I've answers to your answers;
and questions for your questions."

"And will men follow you for
only questions?"

"Of course they will, for nothing
else will have esteem. Your myths
grow weak when sciences grow strong.
I shall expose you, Anthem—you will
see. I'll ask you in the crowded
market place just how it is that
science is defied by all your magic
claims that executed Singers come
to life again."

When Sarkon stood, he truly seemed
the ideal man, a standard towards
which all men would strive,
what every man would want to be, at
least the ones content with merely
being men.

Then Sarkon snapped his fingers and
called out, "Old Woman, come at once
and stand again alive..."

And Anthem shuddered as he felt his
neck hair bristle. It was
incredible, but standing there beside
the rugged youth was the old woman
who had died before the city well.

"She is dead," stammered Anthem.
"The sexton buried her and I now
have her scroll."

"No, Anthem. Look! She's alive
just as you claim your Great Lover
is alive."

"I see a replica and that is all..."

Anthem stopped his speaking, and
looking up he called for more
authority than he alone possessed.
"Earthmaker, Father of the Singer,
remove the woman's mask and
let us see what treachery this is."

The woman groaned and stumbled to
her knees. At once a hideous strength
fell scaled upon the floor and slithered
over Sarkon's feet. Its green-brown
gills croaked out a strange defiance of
the presence in the life of Anthem.

"Sarkon," he said, "it was nothing
but a trick. It was only a dragon
that you feed in your great pit."

"Perhaps," replied the youth. "But
some who do not know the Singer will
believe this monster is the author
of the scroll you have. Between this
woman and myself will lie a path of
blood for you. You cannot win,
poor Anthem."

"Take your ugly pet and go," he
cried. They left in fiendish laughter
that rattled windows and vanished
in the air.

Then peace acquired the place that
conflict had so lately held, and
stayed the night. Anthem slept.

But Sarkon waited for a student
whose troubled mind and heart had never
met. Sarkon vowed they never would.

IX

Science can change the
compound states of matter
easier than it can change
its mind.

The student known as Everyman was
indeed a troubled youth but grateful for
the wind and rain. Though he often
hungered to be free, he was not among
the thousand who had been unchained.

He accepted all the sciences as truth
but rejected all ideas that Earthmaker
could exist. Yet he sometimes wished
such mystic falsehoods true. For
those who claimed to be unchained seemed
so naive to Everyman. And yet they
seemed to own contentment he had never
managed in pursuing all his sciences.
He could not make himself believe
the Singer was the Father-Spirit's Son.
Nor did he trust the rumor that
the Singer had returned to life.
Yet the Singer haunted all his
idle hours.

Everyman's great appetites were
of the heart. He tried to sate his
hunger by devouring the philosophies
and sciences he loved. He read
the poems of the priests and mountain
gods, but their verses seemed as rigid
as the columns of their temples.

He read the woman's scroll, but
rejected all her rules and altar
laws. And now in the upheaval that
spread outward from the city's walls,
men everywhere rejoiced that the
Singer had returned, and that the
Golden Age had come.

Everyman was reading from a scroll
called the REASON OF EMPTINESS while
he lay on a grassy slope of summer.

"Hello!" called out a voice from
somewhere behind him. "What do
you read?"

Everyman looked up and then looked
back upon his book. He said,
"I read of reason."

"What reason?" queried the approach-
ing youth.

"The reason that teaches Terra made
herself when there were civil wars
among the stars."

"And do you think it true?" the
stranger asked when finally he
reached his side a little out of
breath.

"How can I tell?... Come now...
let us not begin with our philosophies
but with our names... I am Everyman."

"And I am Sarkon!"

"And tell me, Sarkon, do you believe?"

"Yes," said the handsome youth. "I
believe in all I am and nothing else.
I believe in eating when I hunger,
loving when I lust and sleeping when
I weary of the game."

"But of the current madness that

the Father-Spirit has a living
Son who sings?"

Sarkon laughed. "It's a myth
for ignorance to feed upon. You surely
do not seek to be unchained?"
he asked sarcastically.

"A thousand were, they say, upon
the third of Krios, when the Wind
blew."

"And do you think that you should
feel guilty just because the
Singer died?" asked Sarkon.

"No, of course I don't.
It's just..."

"What?"

"Well, those unchained seem filled
with what I lack somehow."

"They are," replied Sarkon. "They
all are filled with madness! Be
grateful that you lack what they
are filled with."

"Perhaps," said Everyman, staring
vacantly into the distant sky.
"Do you believe the Singer came
alive again?"

"No—not at all. I know the man
who buried him, you see. His grave
is in a country field..."

"Then let us go and dig him out

and show the unchained men of Terra
their great folly and absurdity."

Sarkon blushed. "I... wh..."
He stammered much before he finally
spoke. "The grave, I must regret,
lies far away. We have not time enough
to travel there today," he finally
explained. He quickly changed
the subject. "It's just as well,
believe me. Could you, good scientist,
believe that Terra was created when
the Singer sang in open space
and let all matter out of nothingness?"

"No, no. I'll trust the scholars
there. The Singer did not sing to
make the trees. Trees gathered up
their being from the seas. I know
that when we get the gods involved
no scientific issues are resolved.
But then why do I hunger for
more than I am fed from all the
scrolls of science?"

"You hunger," Sarkon said, "for
something else. Come, let us fill
our bellies so our minds will not
be restless, nor our hearts. I
know women who can make philosophy
an elementary matter. When lust has
eaten at the table of desire, you
will be satisfied again. When
the flesh feeds itself, the hunger
of the spirit is forgotten."

Sarkon stood. He was quite practical
it seemed to Everyman, who was tired
of study. Everyman also thirsted for
the taverns of the city where he and

Sarkon could forget their emptiness
of soul.

Everyman then stood, and as
he stood he said, "Let's go and
worship at the temple of indulgence
till all our appetites are full..."
And then he added, "Tomorrow, Sarkon,
could you take me to the man you spoke
about—the man who laid the
Singer in his grave?"

Sarkon looked away and paused, but
finally he said, "Tomorrow, I will
take you there."

X

At stonings angels stand apart
And weep above the martyrs' groans.
But demons always grin, and keep
Both hands grasping—filled with
   stones.

As Sarkon and Everyman came through
the city gates a street minstrel was
singing to a crowd. Sarkon despised
the poor who listened to the balladeer.

"Do you know the man who sings?"
asked Everyman.

"His name is Anthem," answered
Sarkon with no apparent interest.

"Isn't he the street singer who
sang the day the wind came from
the mountain?"

"He is. But careful, friend, or he
will have your science in his pouch.
You'll be dancing to his tunes."

They passed so near the street singer
they could hear the verses of his
song.

"Come to the Singer you science-stained.
Cry for the crime and be unchained
Here in the great Invader's reign."
The people who watched him as he
sang joined him in his simple melody.

Sarkon reached down and found
a heavy stone and hurled it.

The rock struck Anthem's forehead
such a blow he almost fell unconscious.
The song abruptly stopped. The little
group of street balladeers closed around
him as a shield.

Everyman, incensed by Sarkon,
turned on him and shouted:
"Why did you do that?"

"He sings a lie," said Sarkon.

"But still he is a man... Have you
some grudge that makes you hate him?
Are there reasons other than his song?"

"None. Come, the tavern is a better
place to talk," said Sarkon.

As they were leaving, Anthem was
revived, and Everyman could hear him
singing once again:
"Come, Terra. Let us sing of love
And the broken hand in the ragged glove.
For ours it is to be set free,
Unchained and given destiny."

"How can he sing?" thought Everyman.
He wanted to turn back, but he placed
his hand on the latch to the tavern door.

XI

Love is substance. Lust, illusion.

Only in the surge of passion

Do they mingle in confusion.

Dawn came swiftly on the eve of
lust. When Everyman awoke his
head was on the bosom of a maid.

"Did I satisfy you, Everyman?"
she asked.

"Last night you did," he answered.
"But now I hunger once again."

"For food or love or books?" she
asked in deep sincerity.

"For none of these. For something
more, if something more there be." And
then he asked, "Where is my young and
god-like friend? Still with his maid?"

"Which maid? Five went to him last
night. His science is his appetite—
ever eating, never full."

"Did he say that?" asked Everyman
in disbelief.

"Oh no," the maid replied. "The
thought was mine. He is a handsome
rogue, but every night he prowls the
taverns of the street and preys upon
such souls as he may meet. Few tell
him no. It's strange. Few like him,
though none resist him long. He never
drinks or sleeps alone... Do you
like him, Everyman?"

"Well, no. I guess not," he said,
"though I never thought of it till

now. Tell me, maid, do you know a
balladeer named Anthem?"

"The crazy man, who sings to rabble
in the streets?"

"You know him then?
Where does he live?"

"Why, right above this tavern,"
she replied.

XII

Appetites ignored revolt
and break the windows of the
shops to get at food.
But hunger of the soul
grows weak with malnutrition
and begs a crust
of spirit.

The steps that waited on the upper
room were old and rickety. But
Everyman ascended them . . . hesitated . . .
and knocked.

"Come in," said Anthem as he opened
wide the door. "Are you not Sarkon's
friend?" he asked.

"As he has friends," he said and then
went on. "I cannot tell you why I've
come, and yet I feel those who threw
their stones at you were evil men."

The new scar glistened even in the
scanty light of Anthem's room. "Sarkon's
an ugly man and capable of ugly deeds."

Everyman was puzzled. "I thought
Singerians never criticized another man."

Anthem could not bring himself to share
with Everyman the truth. He knew the
young man could not believe it all
so soon.

"You did not come to dress my
wound or tell me you were sorry
for the injury."

"No, I have come because I've
gorged and baptized every appetite
in full indulgence and I am
hungry still," said Everyman.

"Earthmaker has a living Son who
fills all emptiness above the brim."

"So I have heard, yet I have
evidence—the Singer is a fraud.
Tonight the riddle will be solved,
for I will meet the man who laid
your Singer in the grave. He
put his mangled body in the ground
the night the great machine fell
off the wall and nothing has dis-
turbed his grave . . ."

"Did Sarkon promise you the
introduction?" Anthem asked.

"He did, in fact," Everyman replied.
"The digger of the Singer's grave
is his close friend."

Anthem was puzzled by the proposition.
What was Sarkon's hope in using such
a falsehood? He walked to a table piled
high with scrolls and scratched some
hasty words on a piece of parchment.

"Here, when you meet the digger of
the Singer's grave, open this folded
scrap of paper and read aloud the
words. But do not open it or read
it till then."

"I do not understand."

"You may quite soon," said
Anthem. They left the room together
and stepped into the streets.
Anthem began to sing.

And Everyman went back to the
fields to study science and hope
Sarkon would come by early afternoon.
He was not disappointed.

XIII

A magician pulls
bunnies out of empty hats.
An Evil Lord pulls reptiles
out of dank and crawling pits and
places writhing, muddy serpents
in the cradles of the infant saints.

When Sarkon appeared, he
was naked to the waist. The muscles
of his shoulders glinted bronze
beneath his strong neck and bold
head. He bore a discus with the
arrogance of self-assurance.

"Sarkon!" Everyman exclaimed.
"You are a god indeed!"

"Ah, ah, ah," the handsome youth
responded. "The gods are dead,
remember? Now there is only
science and yearning appetite.
How did you find your maid last
night?"

Everyman looked down. "I only
loved her while I lusted, and then
I hated her for making me recall
I am never satisfied for long."

"What are you reading from your
sciences today?" the churlish
Sarkon probed.

"Today I'm reading the scroll called
THE REASON OF SUBSTANCE. Did you
know that this small stone I prop
my foot against is a seething mass
of whirling orbs, each with its tiny
lightning storms and milky ways?"

"So I have heard, Everyman. And
are the tavern maids composed of
such minutiae—of dancing, shooting
particles of stars—of spinning

microworlds tearing orbits in the
center of their bosoms, and fleet-
ing beams of small galactic storms?"

"You've read the scrolls of science!"
said Everyman in glee.

"Enough to know that we are but a
gathering of microsuns, fast
moving asteroids that whirl at
lightning speed. But evening's
soon and we must get to the
taverns once again."

"Before we go, you promised me an
introduction," Everyman reminded
him.

"I did?"

"Yes. You said that I might meet the
man who laid the Singer in his grave."

"Oh yes . . . him." Sarkon grimaced
and then with added certainty he
acquiesced, "Very well, young scientist.
You shall meet the man indeed. He's
buried many singers I can tell you,
friend. His shovel never rusts.
Come right this way."

Everyman still marveled at the handsome
Sarkon, looking yet as though some
sorceress had blessed a statue in the
temple and set it free to tread the
planet and give the gaping men of Terra
an exhibition of divinity. Then
Everyman remembered that in his view
of things, there were no gods—oh, how
he wished there were!

He followed Sarkon down a rocky
path into a grove of trees where
the afternoon sun fell in splotches
on the ground. In the scarcity of
light he saw an old man sitting by
a rough wood shack. As he looked
upon the old man, he felt once more
the crumpled parchment in his pocket
and wondered if there would be ample
light to read it when the time
should come.

"My lord Sarkon," said the old man.

"Shhh!... " said Sarkon in reply.
"I've brought a visitor with me
today."

Everyman cupped his hand before his
mouth and whispered to his handsome
friend, "Why did he call you 'lord'?"

"He's an old fool," Sarkon answered.
And then he said, "Old Man, this is
a friend of mine... Let's not pretend
this afternoon. He wants to know if
you're the man who laid the Singer in
his grave?"

"I am, my lord Sarkon." The old man
turned his head away and fidgeted: He
had used the forbidden word again...
"Yes, I took him from the wreckage of
the great machine and buried him in a
rocky field not far from here."

"But," protested Everyman, "the
Singer's followers all say his body
was never found though all the wreckage

had been searched. In fact, they teach
he came alive again."

"They are liars," the old man said.
"I buried him and two weeks later
his grave was as I left it. He
still is there. Here's all of him
that I have left." The old man pulled
a broken lyre from beneath the crude
wood bench he sat on.

"Somehow I sense," objected Everyman,
"that you are right and all Singerians
are fools, but I can see so little
falseness in them. I think they
do believe they tell the truth."

"I tell you," argued the old man, "I
buried him and he is dead, and all
Singerians are liars and fools."
Each successive word expressed his
rising anger.

To Everyman the time seemed right to
pull the parchment from his pocket.
Sarkon shifted his weight from
one foot to the other as Everyman
read the strange words:
"In the name of Earthmaker,
Father-Spirit of the Singer,
be what you really are!"

They were strange words indeed to
Everyman, but no sooner had he
read them than the old man fell
forward on the broken instrument.
For a moment he lay silent on the
ground. Then an ugly reptile
lay in the old man's place. The

dragon hissed and moved toward
Everyman.

Bolt upright, Everyman stood stiff
and ceased to breathe.

Sarkon was silent, then he cleared
his throat and the dragon disappeared.

Everyman relaxed and regained
his composure, then asked, "Sarkon,
why did the old man call you 'lord'?"

"Come, Everyman. The taverns open
soon."

"No, Sarkon. I have seen what I
needed to see. The scrolls
have not allowed such things for
me. Yes... now I've hope. Your
monster set me free. For if the
dragons live, the gods may be.
Lust alone tonight, Sarkon.
I do not know if the Singer is alive,
but I do know this: Your old friend
never buried him."

Sarkon burned with anger as he
walked away. He took five steps,
stooped down, picked up a rock
and hurled it with more than
human force.

The sky swirled and the blood
ran warm across the face
of Everyman. He slumped to the
ground unconscious, and in his
great delirium were sweeter dreams
than he had ever dreamed before.

In the mist of his concussion swam
wondrous dragons and singers
in the streets.

Sarkon would have killed him
for the dreams if he had known
the nature of his sleep. But he
had other appetites to feed. There
were tavern maids and other youthful
scientists he labored to deceive.

XIV

I heard the ballad of a fool
whose simple song made synonyms
of life and death and cursed the
right and called it wrong:
    Come play along the precipice—
    Don't worry that the cliff is steep—
    The little flowers on the brink
    Are daisies, but their roots
        grow deep.

The Invader stirred within the drowsy
Anthem and he could not sleep. He
pulled his tunic on and then his
shoes and hurried out into the night.
His feet were given no instruction
by his mind and yet they fell in
firm intention. At last the meadow
hurried into trees and soon became
a grove so dense the starlight
halted on the tops of leaves.

He felt his way along in some
denial of the mission that he
could not comprehend, till in
a clearing where no star shade
fell, he saw a man lie wounded
in the night. He approached and
knelt in dust to lift the youthful
head which lay face down on the earth.

In a nearby stream he soaked his
shirt, then lifted up the head
and swabbed the dust and blood
away. It startled him to realize
the man in need was Everyman.

When he had swabbed the face the
second time, the youth awoke and
muttered from the mist that was his
mind. He sat upright and stared
into the night. When finally his
world merged with the one he sought
to see, he knew the hand that cooled
his brow was the singer that Sarkon
had stoned in his contempt. They
shared a common wound. At last words

broke the stillness of the woods.
Night silence surrendered up its hush.

"There are dragons!" said Everyman.

"Yes..."

"The old man did not put the Singer
in his grave!"

"No..."

"Why did you come?"

"The Invader led me to you
because the Singer loves you."

"Are the Singer and the Invader one?"

"As water and ice are one—or
heat and fire. The Singer came
to be a man, then came again
to be in man. The first time
that he came he was the Troubadour
and the next, the Wind Song."

"Why did the old man change himself
into a dragon?" asked Everyman.

"He did not."

"But I saw him do it here...
tonight... He changed himself
into a croaking evil thing."

"That's only as it seemed. It was
a dragon who had changed himself
into a man. The words you read
from the parchment scrap forced
him to become what he has been

through all time. A man can not
become a dragon. But a man may
sometimes be a dragon in disguise."

"But here tonight, he called
Sarkon his lord."

"Sarkon is his lord—he is the
lord of all dragons. And every
monster has the power of masquerade.
Sarkon himself loves the masque and
now he plays the role of mountain
god. The first time we met he was
a piper who played an evil song
to drive me mad."

"He was a piper then?"

"No more a piper than a mountain god.
He is his cloak, whatever garment suits
his evil purpose."

"And what is his purpose?"

"To smash the world the Father-Spirit
made and loves. He gloried in the
Singer's death and hates the very
thought that the Invader is the lover
of all men. He told you that there
were no gods?"

"Yes."

"He tells others that there are,
but he tells no one that Earthmaker
is the Father of the Troubadour."

"I dreamed in my delirium of dragons
bold and singers in the street. Tell
me of the song," said Everyman.

So Anthem sang in starlight the
Singer's story and when he came
to the Singer's cosmic moments
in the great machine, they both
fell on their knees.

"What must I do to be unchained?"
cried Everyman.

"Cry out your blindness and open
to the Wind."

And Everyman wept into the night
and sobbed his guilt:
"Earthmaker, I regret that your
Beloved died. I put away false
scholarship and pride. Come, Great
Invader! Move inside!"

Once more the radiance grew from the
stars till the Invader had buried them
in gusty hurricanes of brilliance.

And Everyman rejoiced to know the
living Singer who had smashed the
fetters of his intellect and let
his desperation out of hiding.

"I am unchained!" he almost shouted.

"You are indeed!" said Anthem.

"May I have the Stigmon?"

So in the raging light storm of
Invader's power Anthem drew a hand-
ful of the new earth. He traced the
Singer's Sign in the fiery luminescence
of Invader:
"It is only out of Terra's shame

That men of Terra wear the name
Of Singer,
Prince of Planets,
Troubadour of Life . . .
Earthmaker, Singer and Invader be
The substance of infinity."

Everyman surveyed the clot of earth
he held and rejoiced to see the stain
that symbolized the crushing pain
of the machine.

He stared into the glinting radiance
and repeated through half-opened lips:

"O man of Terra, fully know
There is no depth he would not go
To love."

XV

Yes, it was savage for the
rifleman to ask the weeping
mother which of her sons she
would like to have shot first.
But the greater cruelty is
to ask the frightened child
which of his parents he would
least prefer to live.

In the days that followed
Everyman and Anthem became
brothers in the spirit.
Everyman's deep resonance soon made
singing in the streets an eloquent
affair. Daily, as he finished the
Song, men and women, crying out to be
unchained, received the Stigmon.
Everyman offered it in the mystic
magnetism of his melody:

"It is only out of Terra's shame
That men of Terra wear the name
Of Singer,
Prince of Planets,
Troubadour of Life."

And he seemed to have a haunting
subtle light behind his eyes, while
the new earth fell from the hand
of the unchained:
"Earthmaker, Singer and Invader be
The substance of infinity."

But the grandest act of love for
the Singer was the Singer's Meal.
Everyman ate the crushed bread and
remembered the machine where the Prince
of Planets bled. He never tore the
wounded loaves but that he swallowed
hard in joy. Each time they met, they
took the Meal and said,

"And now the great reduction
    has begun:
Earthmaker and his Troubadour
    are one.

And here's the new redeeming
   melody—
The only song that can set Terra
   free.

The Shrine of Older Life
   must be laid by.
Mankind must see Earthmaker
   left the sky
And he is with us... They must
   believe the Song or die."

From day to day they sang the Star-Song
in the streets and ate the Singer's
Meal. In the homes and on the greens
they offered everyone the chance to
let the Great Invader into life. Those
who were unchained from month to month
received the Stigmon.

The days moved on and winter came
and then gave way to spring.
Both Everyman and Anthem went from
time to time into the Great Walled
City and sang the Ancient Star-Song
in the streets. They often saw young
Sarkon near taverns drinking ale with
students as he pointed fingers at the
pair and laughed. Once Sarkon even
sent a group of ruffians who seized
their instruments and harassed them
in the streets.

But not until the month of Krios
did destruction reach its apex.
It happened on a sunny afternoon
that an old woman entered the market
place near the spacious Plaza of
Humanity. She stood and spoke
above the gathering crowd.

"Men of Terra! Remember that our
joy is in the scroll of all the
ages. Our fathers loved this city."
She gestured to the gleaming
bastions of the Great Walled City
of the Ancient King. "But the
followers of the Singer say that men
must not love cities, for Earthmaker
does not hallow stone and mortar.
They cry against the songs the Grand
Musician sings before the shrine of
Older Life. They call our children to
despise our customs and our creed.
They say the recent rains have come
because the Great Invader came to end
the drought of desperation. They teach
that the Great Invader is the spirit
of their Singer whom we hanged upon
the battlements.

"They say the Singer lives and men
should turn aside our heritage and
follow him. They Lie! They Lie!"
she cried.

The crowd grew restless as she poured
contempt on all the Singer's followers,
who seemed to fill the highways and
the market places.

"I am the Keeper of the Scroll, yet
Anthem and the heretic called Everyman
tell everyone that I'm a croaking
dragon from the pit. They sing that
men must turn from me and follow
him who died and lives," she
screamed in fury.

"They tell our youth they must reject
the Scroll of Ancient Truth and follow

these young rebels who try to turn
poor Terra upside down with lies.

"They must be stopped. They are
vermin in the temple of our glorious
ancient truths.
Let vermin die
Or truth shall lie
Destroyed by our
Own apathy
Towards the Shrine
of Older Life.

"They must be driven out," she
rasped. "All who teach that
I am dead and thus to be despised
... Let's strike down Everyman
and his agnostic crowd, till all men
believe again that I do live and
hold the only scroll of truth."

Quickly Sarkon volunteered to lead
the group into the heresy-infested
ghettos of the city. As they moved
through the streets, many in the
angry crowd picked up stones.

"Where is Anthem?" said Sarkon to
a little singing group they
encountered in the streets.

"We know not, brother," answered
all the young Singerians.

"Do you believe the woman is alive
and that she owns the great brown
scroll of the only truth there is?"
Sarkon probed.

"No," replied a youth in simple

openness. He did not know the storm
his honesty was shortly to unleash.
"No, I don't . . . She died a year
ago before a village well. That
bent old woman is a dragon
from the pit."

"Blasphemy," croaked an old voice
in Sarkon's retinue. Sarkon grabbed
the young man by the throat and
screamed in red contempt,
"Infidel! You dare to call the
mother of our faith a dragon from
the pit?"

He struck the youth, who staggered
backwards with such force he fell
across an old Singerian who was
kneeling in the dust. They both
sprawled in the street.

"And you, old man. Do you believe
the Singer is alive?" Sarkon shouted
down in anger.

"I do!" the man replied before the
strong and brutish foot of Sarkon
fell with crushing force into his
abdomen. Sarkon kicked him
again full in the face. Blood
from his mouth coursed through
his silver beard. Unconsciousness
delivered him from pain.

In fury then the crowd that Sarkon
led fell on the group of singers
with clubs and stones. A little
girl who saw her mother bludgeoned
grasped her bosom just before
a flying stone in mercy made her sleep.

When the assailants had withdrawn, no
singers moved for most of them were still
unconscious in the street. Then some
began to stir, each reaching out to
others and offering strength and help.

Two never rose. The old man
hemorrhaged and died. The woman
who received the crushing blow
lingered till the night, then
peacefully she died. When her daughter
woke, she cried.

"Have you a father, little girl?"
an old Singerian asked. Her vacant
eyes said no. "I'll find someone
to care for you. Come with me
tonight," he said.

When word of the assault reached
Everyman and Anthem, the awful burden
of the Song began to settle on their
leaden hopes. The lamp burned low
while they groaned the pain that
seared their souls. They saw the ugly
storm they knew would come by day.
They ached in knowing those who
died were but the first. The Star-
Song stuck in their throats, and
nothing issued out except a lamentation:

"Oh, Father-Spirit, Father-Spirit:
Must truth be vanquished by the lie?
Must orphans watch their mothers die?
Must children whimper, old men sigh
And groan? Hear us for we cry!"

As they lifted up a crushed loaf of
bread to share the Singer's Meal,
light began to flood the table where

they sat. The Invader swept
throughout the darkened room till
every niche was born in brilliance.

Anthem and Everyman fell upon their
knees. Fire played upon the plaster
of the lamp-smudged wall and where it
danced, a vision grew. In the vision,
a behemoth red dragon, chained by his
great clawed feet, stood among such
temples as Anthem had not seen before.
But Everyman knew them well. Behind
the dragon, he could see the giant
gates of Urbis.

While they watched in horror, the beast
devoured a peasant. Then presently
the monster roared and leered
from Urbis into the very souls of
Everyman and Anthem. For a moment
the dragon looked like it would leave
the vision and walk into the little
room they kept. It leered from Urbis,
yet stared into their souls. Then
presently it froze, turned to stone,
toppled and lay dead.

Everyman and Anthem beheld themselves
beneath the dragon armed with bloody
swords. The vision fell away.

The Invader stirred warm inside
them, as the brilliance faded
till all the light was gone, except
for one small lamp that burned on
the table where they sat.

"Do you know the city that we saw?"
asked Anthem.

"Urbis!" said Everyman.

They knew that they must leave the
village near the Great Walled City
of the Ancient King.

Their destiny lay across the
Silver Sea in the city of the West.
Urbis, capital of Terra, a city
where the old woman and her scroll
had never been believed.
Urbis, the shining temple-city
of all the mountain gods.

They consorted with the leaders
of the Singerian Choirs and then
made ready for their voyage.

Months like foam flew by beneath the
keel. Krios came and went but not
their zeal. The Song thrived well in
salt breeze and halcyon seas.

XVI

If Death and Life should ever wed,
There'd be no dynasty.
Their house would fall.

For Death would offer nothing
On his rigid firm demand
That Life must give up all.

The night hung close to the sea.
It seemed to Anthem that the sky
and sea so loved each other that they
merged and left no mark. Thus
often on the trip, Earthmaker and
his Singer merged into a single joy.

During the long voyage, Everyman
and Anthem sang while passengers
and sailors listened to the great
Singer's themes. Several in
the course of weeks cried out to
be unchained. One who sought but
would not yield was Praxis,
the Builder. He labored every
day on a great brown roll of
parchment on which he drew some
clean black lines of stress and
excavation.

"Tell me, Builder, what it is
that you draw," said Anthem.

"These are the plans for the great
temple soon to be built in upper
Urbis," Praxis then replied.

"Is Urbis short of temples?"
asked Everyman in disbelief.

"No. There are temples to all the
mountain gods but none to horses
ever have been built."

"Is yours to be the Temple to the
Horse?"

"Well... yes..." said Praxis.
"At least the unicorn..." Then
formalizing all his doubt he said
with certainty, "It will become the
Gilded Temple of the Unicorn. But
tell me of your Singer, and tell me
what it means to be unchained."

"You may only be unchained if you
renounce your petty dreams and
hunger to be free and come to life.
Then you will know the joy of
melodies that can swirl and echo like a
dervish in the soul," said Anthem.

"Must I give up the mountain gods
to know the Singer's music?"

"Yes."

"But why? Why isn't your Singer
the friend of all the other gods?"
thought Praxis half aloud. He thought
a moment and then continued as if he
had been overcome by a sudden trans-
formation of some lofty thought or
lost ideal. "Better yet, let's give
the Singer temple space in Urbis. I'll
save a handsome niche in the Temple of
the Unicorn where he may stand in state
for all the gods and ages to adore."

Anthem cringed. "No, Builder!...
He is not a mountain god,
for they are not. The Singer is."

"It's all the more a reason that
his reality cannot be threatened
by their non-reality. Let's bring
the Singer to the market place and

raise him in an arch of colonnades.
Let's lift him as a warrior king
in bronze and decorate him
as a slayer of the hosts. Can you
imagine how temple choirs could
sing the Ancient Star-Song in great
antiphonies? Thousands might call
out to be unchained."

He seemed about to cease his
rhapsodizing; then as an afterthought
he added, "He will need a consort
now, of course."

"A consort?" questioned Everyman.

"Yes, to keep him from too much
transcendence: It might destroy
him. Recall the myths. The great
gods never sleep alone or rule alone.
They live in pairs, and in their
heavenly sovereignty they need not
give up such delights as men can
understand. Men will not worship
long that which is too unlike them
or too far above them."

"But that's the meaning of the word
'unchained!' " protested Everyman.
"Freedom only comes when men give up
their grip on their humanity.
Mountain gods are made by men and are
too much men to help. They cannot
liberate who are not free."

The Builder took his pen and dipped
it in the ink and quickly drew a
sketch. It was the Singer as he
imagined him to look—a naked
titan whose great lyre hung

across his back. His heavy locks
of hair fell down over his ears
and sturdy jaws. His thighs were
marble pillars. The drawing was
an athlete god who bore a chilling
likeness to the youthful Sarkon.

He dipped his pen again. This
time he drew a lovely woman, supple-
breasted and yearning in idealism.

"Here," said the Builder, "is the
Singer and his mate. The simple
men of Urbis would worship such a
cosmic pair. Why in their fantasies
the two could romp through starry
constellations and their progeny
would be the infant galaxies. The
ecstasy that they might give the
poor of Terra would truly set men
free."

He stopped again while Anthem
shook his head. In flurried words
the Builder then erupted one
more time. "By the gods, dear Anthem,
we shall make him ride the unicorn.
Think of it! A strident warrior-
troubadour who reigns among the stars
with his great consort Radia. And
when they leave the unicorn to love,
the earth will yield great harvests
of fertility and joy."

"No, Builder!" cried Anthem. "Put
by your gods and unicorns. The Singer
is Earthmaker's only Son. He needs
no temple built by men. Temples
are prisons of both gods and men.

Stone redeemers neither live nor
come again."

"But," said the Builder, "let's edit
him and set him free. Not slay him,
just adapt his small ontology and
give him more humanity that we may
understand, that's all. Change
his solo to a choir and broaden his
small song till all the gods of Urbis
sing along."

Further argument with Praxis would be
to no avail. That both Anthem and
Everyman could see. The voyage soon
would end, and it was clear at least for
now the Singer's friends would not
include the Builder.

The Builder scooped his papers from
the bridge and walked away. The night
drew close; so therefore did the day.
Shortly after dawn, a sailor yelled
the sighting of their destiny. When
Anthem raised his head to look, great
golden Urbis floated on the sea.

Two left the ship to sing in
city streets that very morn. But
in one mind, the Singer sat astride
a unicorn.

XVII

Thank God the priests are dead
and stenographers type memos
where machine-gunned clerics bled.
We were surprised to hear that
the revolutionaries were atheists.
It should not have surprised us as
it did. We had forgotten that the
rabble teemed the lower city and
walked in rags and prayed to St.
Basil year by year. But the Saint
was far too busy with the Czars to
hear. It cost St. Basil everything
to be so uppity.

The Singerians were not so new to Urbis as Anthem first had thought. Some isolated groups of singers were here and there in Urbis but always in the lower city.

Lower Urbis was a tunneled plain where lived the multitudes of dispossessed. They were the secret of the commerce of the upper city where lived the Poet King and all his complex court.

Anthem mingled in the tunnelways of lower Urbis and listened to the superstitions of the laundresses, confectioners and old bootblacks who labored there. They talked in envy of the world above them, the glistening city in the sun.

Some told of leopards near the throne. Some thought the Poet King had access to a gilded door that opened on a magic flyway to the mountain of the gods. Most in lower Urbis did agree that the Poet King was mad. Some said he was a cannibal who glutted every night on the flesh of infants kidnapped from the cradles of the lower city. There were other rumors more bizarre, but Anthem listened long enough to know he'd listened long enough.

Upper Urbis was a sea of great white buildings that dazzled every visitor.

The temples and the senates and the
fountains were a sunlit demonstration
that those who lived in upper Urbis
were Terra's greatest souls.

Fear stalked both cities. Lower
Urbis feared upper Urbis for its
wealth and power. Upper Urbis
feared the tunnel dwellers
for the sheer weight of numbers.
Those in upper Urbis had their
dreams of horror, and in those dreams
the holes that led down to the lower
city swarmed with human insects
coming blind and powerful into
light—the vermin of the night
who lusted for the wealth above them.

Those who roamed the lower labyrinths
had long since given up their worship
of the mountain gods. The white temples
were the altars only for the cultured
and the rich. The upper-world elite
maintained the shrines, for they had
bread. The lower city worshiped only
bread and had no gods, nor wanted them.

Therefore when the Star-Song came
from eastern immigrants a year before,
it met the hapless lives of outcasts
in boroughs of the lower city. They
long had hungered for a god who could
stomach all their sunless miseries
and found such a deity in the Singer
and his Song.

Thus Everyman and Anthem sang
within the dripping caverns of
the underground, and multitudes
of lower Urbis were unchained.

Sometimes the knighted class above
would hear their songs coming full
and free from the passageways beneath.

Before a year had passed the Singerians
heard tales that in the East their
brothers paid for melodies in blood,
and it seemed that only time could
forestall the coming storm in Urbis,
too.

When the Singerian Festival of Life
was past and celebration slept, Anthem
saw a sign written in the language
of the West and posted near all
temples in the upper city.
    ATHEISM IS A CRIME
    PUNISHABLE BY DEATH.
He knew what theologians in the
upper city meant by atheism:
Atheism was disbelief in the
mountain gods. He feared the signs
the more because he knew that most of
his brothers in the boroughs could not
read them.

For a while the signs meant nothing.
The Singer's bands stayed clustered in
the tunnels where even the police of
upper Urbis feared to go. And the Song
passed from passageway to passageway
while seasons in the upper lands tumbled
over one another. More and more of the
tunnel dwellers cried to be unchained.

Each new Singerian received the Stigmon
in the dim light of lower Urbis. And
when the earth fell from their foreheads
and their hands, the words of the rite
echoed through the caverns:

"It is only out of Terra's shame
That men of Terra wear the name
Of Singer,
Prince of Planets,
Troubadour of Life . . .
Earthmaker, Singer and Invader be
The substance of infinity."

From day to day they shared
the Singer's Meal and celebrated his
death in the machine. The volume of
their singing grew until the Festival
of Life had come again.

The Festival of Life was the Singerian
holiday that marked the hallowed day
Earthmaker breathed into his executed
Son the breath of life. The Troubadour
was no longer Terra-bound. He had
come in pain to break the old and
obsolescent definitions of the dead.
The word "dead" was now taboo,
and those who were unchained considered
it obscene.

In the dancing and the singing of the
Festival of Life, a guardsman of the
Poet King had heard the joy and entered
the tunnels in disguise. Whatever
his intentions were, he found himself
compelled by great intrigue and the
Invader drew him into life. He fell
upon his knees and cried to be unchained.

In the weeks to come he sang discreetly
in the taverns and the halls of upper
Urbis and several in the very palace of
the Poet King became unchained. Their
atheism kept discretion and the Star-

Song moved in subtle circles of their
confidence.

Joy came to the upper city. Those
who knew the Song worshiped in the
labyrinthine covert ghettos
of the lower world. And more and more
they came, till the great Star-Song
was sung by many in the upper streets.

XVIII

Unicorns are garish horses void
  of browns and grays.
We let them live because we fear the
  humdrum in our days.

Look beneath the bloody beams of
  history and find
There is but one alternative to
  unicorns. The mind
May search for more in vain.

"They are here," said Sarkon to the
Poet King of Urbis, "and they are
singing their strange songs against
the mountain gods. Yes, now they
sing in the upper and the lower
city and teach their strains of
atheism in the shadows of the
temples. Their teachings come encased
in catchy melodies that leave their
converts in a state of joy, and
crying out to be unchained."

"Unchained?" asked the King.
"Unchained from what?"

"From fidelity to mountain gods.
They left the East brief years ago, and
now they grow in heavy numbers here
in Urbis too. In the sunless tunnels
underneath us now they multiply like
rats in rotting earth."

Then Sarkon stopped and paced the
marbled flooring before he turned
in venom: "Not only that, O King,
but they insist their music is superior
to all the other poetry of Terra...
Yes... greater than your SONNETS
ON THE CITY or your immortal
EPIC OF THE GODS. They sing
in Terra's underground that no one
but the Singer and his Father are
to be adored and all the other
mountain gods must be despised. And
over all this blasphemy they teach...
I can barely speak their skepticism...

that you, O King, are but a man and
not a god at all."

Sarkon had lost no time in organizing
for resistance in the global capital.
In the few short months since his
arrival, he had brought the artisans
and scientists of Urbis to support the
traditions of the age. This was his
bold attempt to seek the audience and
power of Urbis' throne. He knew that
his performance must be polished and
convincing.

The King began to tremble slightly
as Sarkon spoke. Finally, he lifted
up his head and shook himself and
stood. At length he spoke.

"Is it true that Praxis, the sculptor
and builder, offered this strange Singer
a sacred niche in the Temple of
the Unicorn and his followers refused
the offer?"

"I too have heard it, and I think
it must be true," said Sarkon in
disgust. "I have heard their bold
Anthem will not let their followers
believe in unicorns at all."

"Not believe in unicorns!" cried a
nearby priest. He traced the sign
of Urbis in the air.

"It is true," said Praxis the Builder,
entering the conversation. "I offered
Anthem a temple niche for a statue
of their leader."

"But why did he refuse?" the King
asked in wonder and surprise.

"Because," replied the Builder, "he
believes there are no gods or unicorns,
and he does not want the men of Terra
to look on the Singer as another of
the mountain gods when they do not
exist."

"Enough!" cried the King of Urbis.
"The time has come to deal with this
blasphemous music loose among the
temples of the truth. Tomorrow I
shall have my knights set poison
to the lower city. And we shall
station soldiers at every tunnelway.
Those who survive will be clapped
in irons. We shall start the Games
of Karnos with the public execution
of all who refuse to confess the King
of Urbis to be god. Sarkon, you shall
be Public Prosecutor. You shall set
the penalty and nature of the punish-
ment for those who dare to disbelieve."

Sarkon, beaming at the King's response,
asked if the King could lead them in
the anthem to the mountain gods which
the Poet King himself had written years
before. The court of Urbis joined in
the music which the King led them to
sing:

"And when the wolf came down
    from the sky
And shook off the stars and left
    them to lie
In a pile of sparkling fire
    to be

The isle where Urbis took
   root in the sea.

And dragons came and took
   the land
And hissed their fire
   forbidding man
To settle in the dragons'
   lair,
The star-corpse isle that
   claws laid bare.

But the peasants prayed.
   Primeval morn
Then came on the horn
   of the unicorn
That pawed the sea and
   tore the land
And gored the dragons
   on the sand.

And where the blood flowed,
   there again
Would grow the souls
   of a thousand men.
A thousand gods were
   also born
On the giant horn of the
   unicorn.''

While they sang the anthem, Sarkon,
who seemed the very incarnation of the
gods, walked out of the hall, pleased
at his new position in the service of
the Poet King. Praxis shortly followed
and soon caught up to him in the street.

"I'm almost finished with my statue
of the unicorn," the Builder said.
"As yet, the figure on his back is

still in uncut stone. I had offered
it to the Singer, but he will have
nothing now to do with mountain gods.
I wonder, Sarkon, if you might consent
to be my model for the rider of the
unicorn. Be mindful that it will
be years before his temple is complete,
but when it is you will be there,
timeless in the stone."

Sarkon agreed to be the model.
Praxis' chisel would leave him
for the generations yet unborn to see.
Sarkon loved his great deception.
The Singer's followers would die
for believing far too much. And those
who called them atheists would die
believing nothing much at all.
But he would play the temple game
with rare delight.

All who refused to kiss the
unicorn would die. The very thought
of Everyman and Anthem bowing at his
marble horse and crying out repentance
for their atheism filled him with
anticipation. He could barely wait
for morning when lower Urbis would
be poisoned. The lucky would die
swiftly in the vaulted fuming caverns.
The rest would live to be the sport
of those who loved the temples
and the bloody Games of Karnos.

"Do you believe in mountain gods?"
Sarkon asked the Builder.

"Of course not," answered Praxis.

"Nor I," responded Sarkon. "Isn't

this a glorious destiny? The labels
are so cleverly applied and misapplied.
All living is called death and truth
is called a lie by liars. Nothingness
affirms itself and substance is denied."

Before long they entered the sculptor's
studio. A great unfinished statue
stood before them.

"How long will this take, Builder?"
Sarkon questioned as he undressed to
sit upon a modeled framework of a
gallant steed. His brutal nakedness
led the Builder to applaud and trace
the sign of Urbis in the air.

"Six months I need to finish," said
the Builder, pointing to the statue.

"And will you promise me your soul
were I to give it to you in the
morning quite complete?"

"Impossible!" the Builder cried.
"But if you think it can be done . . .
well, yes. I'll give you anything
you ask."

"Very well. Leave me and you will
see me clearly in this clot of stone
come morning."

The Builder left and Sarkon gloated
once again that he was soon to claim
the souls of men who trusted both the
mountain gods and the Singer. But
best of all, he also owned the soul
of an artist who believed in neither

and therefore was most vulnerable
of all.

When the sculptor came early to his
studio the next day, he was stunned
by the finished statue. In flawless
polished marble his young friend Sarkon,
god-like and gallant, sat astride
the giant unicorn. Across his back hung
the lyre of the Singer—a divine riddle
in marble. Was he the Singer or
the Anti-Singer? Had he the power
of Earthmaker or the mountain gods
or neither?

The unicorn would bring life to
all those who kissed it in the
wisdom of denial. The unicorn gave
life therefore to traitors. The
rest would die and the dying would
come hard, for giant Tasman jackals
snarled in the pits where they
were kept.

XIX

Urbicide may be as quick as a
  coronary
Or as painful as the cancer ward.
Some cities die very fast:
  Hiroshima, Pompeii, Sodom.
Some cities die very slow:
  Masada, Sparta, Dresden.
Ask Leningrad (which took 900 days
  to die) who was more blest.
They envied Nagasaki for her fireball
  from the West.

Urbicide became the fashion of the
day. Killing lower Urbis was accom-
plished by a dozen knights who entered
the tunnels of the underground near
noon. A torch was set on oil-soaked
leaves of poisonous root moss,
and the smouldering fumes swirled
and eddied through the labyrinth.
The caverns became death chambers where
old Singerians died in rags and children
breathed their final breath. Mothers
clasped infants and fell across them
to shield them from the evil haze.
There was no place or time to sing
the one great melody for which they
lived . . . and died.

Only those within a few steps of
outside air survived, and as they
staggered to the fresh clean air of
day, each was clamped in chains and
taken to the prison yards to await
their sentencing.

Everyman and Anthem were spared the
poisonous caverns of the underground.
They had gone early in the day to
sing in the construction camps where
tradesmen labored with the quarried
stones to move them into columns of the
city's latest temple. From every tunnel
exit they heard the wailing of arrests.
Lower Urbis died by nightfall.

Everyman and Anthem searched for
someplace to wait the coming storm.
They found a small forgotten park,

grown up in weeds, that sheltered an old
grotto in decay. They prayed in silence
for their brothers in the tunnels.

The day was marked by such arrests
as Urbis had never seen before.
Singerians by hundreds were herded
into cells so gorged that there was no
room to lie or sit.

When morning came construction crews
arrived at every opening to the lower
city. The poisoned air was sealed in by
masons who built walls at every entrance.

A brokenhearted Anthem wept.
None who lived were sure who the
survivors were. Nightly as the
sun went down, grief-laden voices rose
from a hundred cells and the Star-Song
floated on the air:

"In the beginning was
    the song of love.
Alone in empty nothingness
    and space
It sang itself through
    vaulted halls above,
Reached gently out to
    touch the Father's face..."

Upper Urbis battened down their windows
to keep the music out, but still it
filtered through the lattices so that
the free men of the city wondered who
was really free. Only those unchained
could know.

The music of a free man taunts
a slave. And the free were found only

in prison cells and tunneled
tombs below. The rest of Urbis prayed
for freedom to the unicorn of life
and tried to sleep. But sleep, like
freedom, came only to the prisoners.

In the weeks that passed before the
Games of Karnos hope began
to circulate among the prison cells.
"The Singer will return and smash the
structures of the state. The Poet King
and Public Prosecutor will be swallowed
by the Canyon of the Damned." Thus
spoke the hope.

On the eighteenth day of the
imprisonment a baby died in cell
fifteen. The mother tried concealing
it but finally slipped it through the
rusted iron grate of her cell door.
She saw her baby moved along before
the shovels which pushed the human
residue into the drayage carts. The
mother cried to the Singerians in her
cell, who were again reminded
of the coming Singer and his promises
of victory.

On the twenty-second day of the
imprisonment a woman became sick in
cube eighteen. Her fever sparked
attempts at quarantines. Within a week
most of the cell was sick. The guards
themselves contracted the contagion and
the fever spread throughout the camp.
The death toll was most severe among
the very young.

The victims of disease were burned.
And so by day the prisoners could see

the smoke columns rise where bodies
burned outside the prison yards.

Seven days before the Games of Karnos
Everyman sent a small scroll wrapped
in a sheath of wax. He gave it to the
sentry with a bribe. The guard slipped
the scroll into a pail of swill and
passed it through the gate in cell sixteen.

A convert finding it, stripped all
the wax away. The scroll was dry.
Its title: THE FINALE!
Its subject: Hope!

"Death cannot be to those who know
The Troubadour of Life. He gives
A crown to every man who shows
By dying that the Singer lives.

So give the breath you cannot keep
To gain the life you cannot lose.
Before the Axman never weep,
But sing with Joy the Singer's truths.

The prince of dragons soon must fall
Before the Prince of Planets."

The scroll told futuristic tales the
prisoners could never fully understand.
Its saga brimmed with beasts and armies
and cities under siege. Most of them
rejoiced at paragraphs they understood.
Urbis, tyrant of Terra, was mentioned by
her ugly name. She would be destroyed
for all her sins, and the Poet King
and Prosecutor would be sentenced at
the throne of Earthmaker.

The scroll was passed from fevered hand

to fevered hand and the Singerians
sang a new hymn, one that spoke of
hope. Most felt the Singer would
return before the dreadful Games
began. And so they sang:

"He comes in power,
Rejoice the hour of
  jubilee is near.
Lift up the cry
Before we die,
  our Singer will appear."

Sarkon made the Builder his chief aide
to organize mass execution of all
Singerians. Three days before the
long-awaited Games were scheduled to
begin, the Public Prosecutor announced
a special mandate to the wardens of
the prisons: "All children in the cells
below the age of seven summers must
be taken from their parents."

This would test their victory and joy.
They lifted up their voices and begged
the Singer come.

XX

It's strange that Spartacus forgot
to tell his brothers in rebellion
that they would all be crucified.
When there are too many crosses
there are none.
A drop of blood is ghastly.
A sea of blood accepted.
We weep above a single dying beast
but whistle past a slaughterhouse.

You are my aide," said Sarkon
to the Builder. "You must be
the one to see the mandate is
carried out."

"But why?" asked Praxis.

"Because the children should be cared
for in a special way before their
parents die in the great stadium.
It hardly seems humane to throw them
to the beasts; they are so young."

"Oh, come now," the Builder then enjoined with mock compassion. "Since
when have you become concerned about
the welfare of children?"

"There is a fear that if the beasts
in the arena seize and devour
a small child they may not even lunge
at those adults we wish destroyed."

"But what of mercy? Do we simply
tear them from their mothers' arms?"

"If they will not give them up in
peace," said Sarkon.

"Peace... peace... No...
I cannot do it."

"You will do it," Sarkon shouted in
growing rage. "I finished up your
unicorn in a night. You promised
me your soul. Have you forgotten,
Sculptor? I own you now."

"But the children?" he protested,
somewhat weaker than before. "The
little children?"

"They are the slime and filth of lower
Urbis. They do not trust in unicorns
or mountain gods. All such atheists
must die."

"But you do not believe in unicorns
or gods and yet you live," said Praxis.

"Nor you, Builder. But your unbelief
will make the job I give you easier.
Look at it this way: If there really
are no gods, there's no morality or
crime. And without gods, what
difference does it make? The children
you slay are a small function of flesh,
tiny claw and organ—a passing movement
in the sea of time. They are machines
which eat the general welfare. In
slaying them, therefore, you are a saint
who stops their pointless eating of the
common good. Yes, Praxis, drag them
from their mothers and do not spare
them for their screams. Here are your
orders for the prison wardens."

Praxis was ripped by shame, and burned
in furious hatred towards Sarkon, but
he took the scroll and left.
The children would be placed in the
chambers of a cave and poisoned in
the fumes of root moss.

Praxis trudged the heavy furlongs to
the prison yards in agony of soul—
a soul that he no longer owned. He had
decried all serious belief. Now he had

grave doubts about his doubts.

Once in the prison, he read the orders
from the scroll and shouted to the
crowds that huddled in the cells:
"Every child of less than seven summers
must be yielded up. You have the
promise of the state that they will die
most mercifully in the caverns of
Karnos."

A flood of agony swept through the
cells. There were no tears, just
stunning disbelief. Shock tore the
tongue of desperation from the hour
of doom. Mothers drew their little
ones tightly to themselves and stared
wide-eyed at the gratings of their
cells.

"Simply pass your children out the
door, as every door is opened, one
door at a time. Don't try escape or you
will die ahead of time, and your children
will not die in mercy but be clubbed
before your eyes."

Praxis hated his decree. And he hated
Sarkon. But more than all he hated
Praxis. He wished the Singer really
were alive and would come and strike
him dead and save them from this hour.

The door to cell one was opened
wide and two small forms were laid
outside—dead. There were red marks
on their necks. They had been quickly
strangled by their mothers. The muffled
sound of weeping blasphemed the
inner-sanctum of the prison. The soul

of Praxis now was gripped by high
compassion that would fold an infant
into gentle death before it laid a
frightened child before such lonely
dying as the executioners of Urbis
could supply.

In cell two a mother without the
strength to slay her son tried
desperately to hold him tight, until
a knight pulled the frightened child
away and bludgeoned his mother with
a mailed glove. He slammed the door
as she fell backward screaming. The
child beheld her mangled face with
terror in his own. Something in the
Builder died.

Praxis cried when cell three was
opened. Three of the children who were
placed outside were strangled. Two
more reached in horror for the parents
they would never see again.

Before the fourth cell opened, a
low and plaintive chorus had begun,
and song spilled into the courtyard,
flooding every cranny of the prison
with the chorus of their hymn of hope.
   "He comes in power,
    Rejoice the hour of
      jubilee is near."

All afternoon the work went on. Most
children laid outside were dead. The
dead were placed on one cart, the living
in a cage with high iron sides. Their
wailing played counterpoint to
the Singer's song of hope.

The crying and the joy filtered through
the souls of guardsmen, knights and
courtiers.

The inmates would have loved to have
the Singer's Meal, but they had no
bread. So as they joined in singing
once again the Star-Song, a radiance
garnered light from torches and
spread in brilliance through the
cells. They sang in brighter light
than any day.

XXI

We have heard that when the
commandant presided at the
execution of the first Jews, he
faltered momentarily. A woman
held up her infant to him, crying,
"Please take my baby." He turned
as though to spare her son the
rifle fire. And then he clicked his
heels and turned away. The next
six million souls were paperwork.
Occasionally he left the office with
a headache, but only because he
feared the gas was running low
or the cattle cars were late.

he unicorn was placed on a little elevation in the Stadium of Life the day the Games began. Hushed singing of the national hymn, the Anthem of the Unicorn, opened the festivities. Singerians were given their last chance to surrender their atheism and salute the great stone horse. Few did.

The events were divided into three separate games, each occupying about an hour. The first games were the Honor Games in which White Knights sought to defend their territory filled with atheists, while Black Knights tried to penetrate their lines and kill the rabble in the lime-chalked boundaries. The last White Knight with Singerians still alive was then declared the winner. Singerians not killed the first day became the victims of the next.

The second event was called the Truth Games. In games of Truth, knights of the unicorn advanced on foot to Singerians and offered them a final chance to recant and confess the true reality of mountain gods. One or two of those who huddled there did indeed recant. The rest were clubbed. The knight with the greatest number of "converts" was declared the winner. The "converts" were not many, but whenever a Singerian kissed the unicorn, a great cheer rose from thousands in the stands. Such Singerians were

spared and loaded into carts and sold
on auction blocks outside the stadium
when the Games were over for the day.

The third event was called Life Games.
In these contests, Singerians were
given a short sword and the right to
live until the morrow if they could
kill the giant Tasman jackals. These
beasts were set on them in pairs. Few
survived. Sarkon was pleased most with
these games which he himself invented
for amusement. He was always in the
stands, smiling over all the carnage
of the Games.

The Builder felt a strange revulsion
as he was seated in the Stadium of Life.
He refused to sing the Anthem of the
Unicorn and thought his protest went
unnoticed in the multitudes of those
around him in the stands.

The Games continued. Sarkon saw
the Builder leave the stands before
the main event. Misery dwelt in
the Builder's heart, and he wandered
as far away from the stadium as he
could. He finally stumbled on an
old grotto covered with vines and
broken beams. He entered in beneath
the shade of afternoon and sat down
silently. He buried his head in his
hands and tried to forget that he
was real. His soul, as much as
it existed, was under evil subjugation.
He wished, like mountain gods, that
he was not.

After several minutes he became aware

of men's voices praying and singing.
They were Singerians but somehow qu ̣
familiar. Suddenly he realized that
Everyman and Anthem were in the grotto
too. In a moment the Singerians were
aware of him whom they had met
so long ago.

Anthem spoke in both surprise and fear.
"Peace, Sculptor! Are we now under
state arrest? We have heard, Praxis,
that you delight in murdering
helpless children."

"It is a lie! Sarkon owns me totally.
I never would have done it but for my
bargain. I traded him my soul for
the statue I wish I never had begun."

"Builder, would you even now be free
of such a bargain, if you could be
free?" asked Everyman.

"There is no hope. Earthmaker, if he
is, must loathe my wretched soul, if
I have one."

"Both Earthmaker and his Singer are.
And you may be unchained if you cry
out your guilt. Accept the Star-Song
and the Stigmon and join us in the
Singer's Meal."

In the distance they could hear the
muffled cheers of upper Urbis as
their brothers died.

"Hear the throng. They perish without
hope. Yet each believes the Singer
will return and rescue him from

death. I envy them even if he should
never come. Dying for any god is
better far than living without one."

"Oh, Praxis, cry out hope and be
unchained while there yet is hope,"
Anthem pleaded.

But Praxis turned and walked away.
He had been gone for just an hour when
Black Knights came to the gateway of
the grotto. Everyman and Anthem were
arrested. Sarkon, who had noticed Praxis
leave the stands, had sent some
knights to follow him. Thus the grotto
was discovered.

Sarkon was delighted at the capture
of the pair and told the Poet King
that the leaders of the Singerian
revolt at last were clapped in irons.

The public execution of Everyman was
scheduled immediately. Anthem was
placed in the cages for the Games.
But Everyman had been the special
grudge of Sarkon. Since he had given
up his science for the Singer, he
would die a special death.

XXII

The son of a hangman will
play with ropes and dream of the
day he will have a scaffold
of his own to tend. But let him
drink too deep of love and he
will only stroke the hemp
and cry that he is man.

Praxis trembled when Sarkon told
him he would be the executioner
of honor. His job was to set
the torch to the oiled faggots at
the feet of Everyman.

"Plague and Singerians must be handled
just alike or they will spread," Sarkon
said. "When he is bound upon the wood,
you only have to take the torch and
plunge it at his feet. Just think,
dear Praxis, you are the doctor of the
sick mentality that eats like cancer
on the great traditions of our state."

"I cannot do it!" cried Praxis.

"We have a bargain . . . I own the
soul you don't believe you have,"
said Sarkon. "And you will burn the
faithless flesh of Everyman—and the
unicorn will guard your way."

"There is no unicorn," groaned Praxis.

But they had been through all that
before. He suffered guilt until the
evening of the execution came. The
knights of Urbis delivered Everyman
and laid him on the wood. The rough
sticks cut into his abdomen and shoulders. A priest of temple twenty-three
put the oil of mercy on his shoulders
to make his dying easier. Then in the
custom of his faith, he spat into the
face of Everyman and spoke the liturgy

of heresy. He rang three silver bells
and walked away.

A priest of temple seventeen led the
crowd of citizens in singing the Anthem
of the Unicorn. When the singing had
subsided, Praxis took the torch and
advanced to the naked unbeliever. As
Everyman and Praxis faced each other
it was clear which one of them was
desperate.

"Please believe in unicorns," the
Builder begged the youthful scholar.
"Believe and I'll not have to touch
this wood with fire. Believe in just
a few of the gods! Kiss the unicorn
and live! Think of me, Everyman! I
cannot live beneath the awful crime
you force me to commit."

"Come, know the Singer's love and
be unchained," said Everyman in
peace. "Yes, come and die
with me and you will know a life
that fire can never touch. You
don't belong to Sarkon. Cry out
to the Singer and you will be
unchained."

Tears glistened in the eyes of Praxis.
He hesitated. And then, instead of
touching the wood with fire, he hurled
the torch at Sarkon and fled into the
thickening gloom of dusk. The speed
with which he acted so surprised the
guards that they permitted him to
leave. Besides, they had no formal
warrant to arrest the master builder
of the state.

By the time that Sarkon picked the
torch and struck the flame, Praxis had
disappeared. Everyman stretched himself
upon the burning wood and died.

Praxis knew Sarkon would waste no time
in finding him. He ran until his
breath gave out, and then he rested
underneath a crannied arch. In tortured
desperation he looked up to the
evening sky.

"Father of the Singer," he implored,
"if you are there, I cry in guilt of
blood and death. In your great heart
can there be love enough to wash from
me the highest crimes of Terra? I
am a wretched, evil man," he sobbed in
violent convulsions. "Oh, Father-Spirit,
if you are, lay me on the wood.
Let Everyman go free."

"Everyman is free!" said a voice
behind him. He cringed to see it
was a White Knight.

"Are you here for my arrest?" asked
Praxis.

"No, I am a Singerian myself. I too
will shortly be arrested. And since I
serve in the King's Guard, I will be
shot by archers. But Everyman is free.
Sarkon only took from him the life no
man can keep to give him one no man
can lose."

"I hunger for the meaning of your
words. I too will die but only
for disobeying Sarkon."

"I saw you throw the torch and followed
you. Sarkon picked up the fire and set
it on the pile of wood, and Everyman
himself became a torch to light the
way to the courts of the Father
of the Singer. Sarkon is afraid.
Each time a Singerian dies in the
Stadium of Life two more leave the
stands. Sarkon fights a futile battle
and he knows it. Even now more than
thirty knights in the Guard of Urbis
believe."

"Don't you mean disbelieve?
Atheism is the charge for which
they die."

"No, Singerians are the true believers.
Don't you see that when they die there
is no emptiness of soul? Only they
are free who die in joy."

"Tell me, Knight, would the Singer
ever ask that children die in
caves?"

The knight, seeing the burden of Praxis'
guilt, asked, "Have you heard the
Star-Song yet?"

"Once when coming to this city
I listened while Everyman sang its
majesty of hope. Then it seemed a
pagan hymn. Now I do not know . . ."
His voice trailed off again.
"I remember just a few lines."

In a low voice the knight began to
sing the words Praxis first heard on
the open sea . . .

"His melody fell upward
    into joy
And climbed its way
    in spangled rhapsody.
Earthmaker's infant stars
    adored his boy,
And blazed his name through
    every galaxy.

'Love,' sang the Spirit Son
    and mountains came.
More melody, and life
    began to grow.
A song of light and darkness
    fled in shame
Before a universe
    in embryo."

The fullness and the quiet of majesty
began to settle on them both. The
Invader came in heavy presence to the
star-hung canopy of crumbled stone.
Mysterious light came gusting through
the ghetto.

As the final strains of the Song faded,
Praxis cried out to be unchained and
the scales of his reluctance fell away.
The awful burden of his crime was lifted
and the Invader, powerful and whole,
swirled light into the darkest fissures
of his soul. Praxis felt the buoyant
delirium of that great discovery that
indeed he had a soul.

"Please, Knight, grant to me the
Stigmon," he pled. The knight picked up
a bit of soil and traced the Singer's
Sign upon the sculptor's face. He
spoke the words of life so glorious

to those who were unchained . . .
"Earthmaker, Singer and Invader be
The substance of infinity."

He and the knight embraced and
parted in the joy he knew was
his forever. He stopped in the
dark street, threw back his head
and laughed a free man's laughter.
He shouted to the stars that had
absorbed Invader's outer light:
"I love you Singer, Prince of
Planets, Troubadour of Life."

And then, he paused and remembered
he was still a part of Urbis and
a servant of the Poet King—or was he?
He turned toward the temples of the
city and shouted fearlessly, "Sarkon,
wherever you are, your grasp of
death is over! I am a Singerian!
Yes, Yes!" he laughed and shouted.
"I, Praxis, am a Singerian!"

None had ever sung it quite so
loudly in the streets of upper Urbis.

XXIII

Creativity can sometimes be a curse.

Ask Dr. Frankenstein.

In half an hour Praxis approached
his studio. Two guards were waiting
at the door. One thing was left to
care for before he submitted to arrest,
and then of course to death.

As he had hoped, the back door was
unguarded. He slipped the key into
the lock and edged the door ajar.
The great leather hinges held their
peace and did not creak. Once in the
studio he felt his way from surface to
surface till his fingers felt
the head of his greatest hammer. He
lifted it in silence from its place
and stole away. The guards in front
were unaware that he had come and gone.

He hurried through the streets until
he came upon the causeway to the
Stadium of Life. The night patrols
recognized him but had not heard he
was a public enemy. Thinking him
the favored aide of the august
Public Prosecutor and Urbis' royal
sculptor, they let him pass. He wound
his way to the ramps that led to the
arena floor and there gilded in
moonlight stood the great statue that
he had made in one long year of toil.

He thought about the weeks it took
to shape the unicorn's great
lifted leg, then drew his hammer back
and heaved it in an arc of power.
The stone leg shattered into silver
shards ignited into sparks by moonlight.

He remembered how the great white
flanks had yielded in the passing
of the months to the urging of his
chisel. Now with brutality he swung
the hammer and a ton of stone came
crashing down. As the body of the
great horse fell, the head of Sarkon
struck the paving and rolled free.

The patrols rushed in when they
heard the raucous clatter of the
statue in disintegration. Praxis
raised his hammer once again and
brought it down on the severed head
of Sarkon. The god-like jaw split.
The heavy forehead shattered.

Praxis was arrested in the marble
wreckage of the unicorn. Even as
the guards held the sculptor fast,
he looked up at the empty stands.
The veins of his neck stood out.
He sang with power.

"And now the great reduction is begun:
Earthmaker and his Troubadour are one."

The stands of the great stadium were
silent in the starlight.

XXIV

The day of one's death is
a good day to be really alive.

The sunlight was blinding as the Life Games began. Anthem and Praxis were the main event and thus released to die at once. They issued under guard from the darkened passageway that led from underneath the lower stands. The grate lifted and closed behind them.

Blinking in the dazzling light, Anthem saw the grinning Sarkon in the royal box with the Poet King himself. But Anthem had grown weary with the ancient struggle. His mind went back to the wall where first he met the World Hater, now the gloating Sarkon, Public Prosecutor. Not many years had gone, but his eyes had beheld all the human savagery that he could tolerate. The letting of his own blood he knew to be the grim necessity for opening the last grand gate of life.

Anthem and Praxis advanced to the center of the ring and knelt. The grating on the west flew open and the giant Tasman jackals leapt into the sun.

Urbis in the passing of the years became the lair of wolverines. And in the crawling centuries her temples crumbled. Terra waited for her final fate. In a day that none could know the Singer triumphed and the mountain gods were all forgotten.

But Sarkon lived and changed his

face and promises for every
generation. And centuries ran down
like wax into some lost abyss.

Then time threw orbit wires around
the planet Terra and silver-suited
men looked out through domes of glass.
And in the center of the universe
the Singer and his Father spoke of
final victory. The ancient World Hater
heard their whispered plans and trembled.

The Prince of Dragons gazed through
a thousand fields of stars, and
across the gleaming universe he saw
the Prince of Planets and steeled
himself for conflict. The light
of the Invader glinted from the
Singer's Sword. A great galactic
storm was gathering among the stars
and Terra lay directly in the wake.

THE
FINALE

I

When worlds cease to roll
old orbits soon become
shallow star tracks
filled with cosmic trash
and planet crumbs—the
final will and testament
of human genius.

The Singer felt a chilling wisp of air pass through the vacuum. He stood upon an asteroid and gazed upon the Center Star, still bright with fire for all its years.

Terra lumbered slowly through the radiance. She looked tired. The Singer's eyes softly saddened as he remembered her once glorious past.

He thought back on that desperate day he felt the cables on his wrists and begged the world cease its senseless murdering of love. The weary planet almost stopped, then rolled slowly on to plod the silver track before it.

"It is her final trip!" a voice behind him said.

He did not need to turn around. He knew who had followed him to his pedestal in space.

"Her very last!" agreed the Troubadour.

"Do you remember, Singer, the last day we spent together there?" World Hater asked.

"It was the day I..." He stopped and looked at his hands, "the day I knew the greatest pain of men. It is hard to call to mind that I died..."

"The day I marked your hands," the Dark Prince finished the thought.

"Now we must go back," the Singer said. "Terra must swelter in the final fiery war. Her death will grieve the Father Spirit."

"No need to grieve. Microworlds die every day," sneered the old antagonist.

"Yes, but dying worlds are to be grieved, and this small mass is held in high esteem: she is Earthmaker's special love, and now . . ."

Again the World Hater finished the words: " . . . and now she dies a glorious death of hate in a bloody war that resurrects my joy in universal bitterness. Destruction and decay shall pave her way to nothingness." He laughed.

The Singer spoke above his laughter: "The time has come. What we began before the Great Tribunal must be resolved."

"Yes, now, out on the Plains of Man, in the bright new capital of Ellanor."

The Dark Prince stretched his arms outward into space. A flame exploded on his hand. Its amber incandescence flickered on his smirking face. "I'm going down," he said, gesturing with his blazing hand toward a range of snowcapped mountains, "to the Caverns of Death."

He rolled the flame into a sphere
between his heavy palms and hurled
it away toward Terra like a meteor. It
was all but lost to sight when it struck
the planet, lighting up the desert
where it fell.

"Ah, Troubadour, it is time for war.
At last my ancient lust for blood
shall have the banquet it desires."

He drew his cape in a great wide arc
and was gone.

The Singer gazed once more upon the
globe. Then looking starward, he
strummed his lyre and sang a requiem:

"Oh, Terra, Terra! I have
     loved you so,
And sown your golden fields
     with songs of peace.
I died to hear the music you
     should know
By now . . . The Song to bid your
     surging cease.

"Why, Terra, did you turn to
     hate? Infect
Your blue and earthen hope
     of joy with
Sin and greed? Earthmaker's
     love was wrecked
On your restless need for
     death and war.

"I'm coming once again through
     battlefields,
To let you know how much I
     care. I'll bear

A gentle sword whose wounds
  will heal—
Embrace you in the flaming
  carnage—share your final
  hour.

"As I once died, you too must
  pass away.
But trust my singing promise
  as your own.
My melody shall sound above
  the fray
Of battlefields: you shall
  not die alone."

He finished the requiem and turned
away, stepped off the silent asteroid
and disappeared in lingering chords
that haunted cosmic emptiness.

A passing comet swept the skyway
and hurried off in dread.

II

When the heavens finally dissolve
and the sound of splintering suns
grows deafening around colliding
worlds, some prophet will be
found extolling hope while fissures
crack the ground beneath his feet.

Beware, O earth, the prophet who
claims to know the time but
never wears a watch.

The cities stood erect. Their windowed obelisks once were pyramids of light. But light had dimmed.

After ancient Urbis fell, Singerians multiplied till every portion of their world held shrines dedicated to the Troubadour of Life.

Now they knew that Terra's life imprisonment was nearly done. They had studied THE FINALE—that book which once had passed through the labyrinths of lower Urbis. They knew their empty rides around the Center Star would soon be through. They saw at hand the tragic, comic ending of their world.

The War of Fire had come.

Yet war was old. It had wounded history for centuries. Armies trained for letting blood, and blood had flowed from battleground to battleground across the grieving years. The War of Fire would be the end of war, for when it came, the storms of flame would reach around the planet and set the very seas ablaze.

Men had come to know the doctrines Everyman debated. Terra knew at last that she was round—that all her oceans froze in pillared ice, where arctic seas rose up in frigid death.

Her mines contained a cold and evil
ore hidden a thousand feet beneath
the ice fields of the Crystal Range.
Brought to light the metal burst
into caustic flames that fed upon
the flesh of men. Men feared that the
ore of death would write the universal
end upon the days.

Elan, Emperor of Ellanor, owned the
mines and stored the ore in mountain
arsenals.

The upper chambers of his mines,
long since stripped of ore, were used
for other purposes. Some served as
quarters for the miners; many were
gaping caverns, eerie and empty.

Some Singerians worked in the mines
and often met to keep the Singer's
Meal and read THE FINALE, their
book of hope.

Dreamer was a miner. He had heard
the Star-Song on his journey to the
Crystal Range several years before.
Invader swirled light into his deepest
crevasses of doubt, and he was
unchained from deep servitude to
the Dark Prince. Now he drove his
mattock into the walls. He knew his
work set him against the life of
Terra, but he found refuge from his
guilt in the great Invader's light.

Dreamer suffered from a malady that
made him an uncertain resident
of two separate worlds. A queer

enchantment had first come over him
while he ate the Singer's Meal. He
dreamed of a glorious realm of life.

He loved the dream and it returned.
Gradually dream usurped reality.
He rose to levels of existence his
Singerian brothers could not
understand. The unbelieving miners
ignored his noble fantasies.

But in the dreams Invader's storms
of light obliterated all drudgery—
transporting Dreamer to walk another
world.

III

The world is poor because
her fortune is buried in the sky
and all her treasure maps
are of the earth.

Some miners near the upper
shafts dressed in heavy furs to fight
the frigid winds of the Crystal Range.
But Dreamer dug in warmer unlit
crevasses a thousand feet below. He
picked the soil to find the fabled
ore of death.

Dreamer's malady worsened, pushed
him to the border of sanity. If he
closed his eyes, the darkness of his
voluntary blindness yielded light.
And when the light had run its way
through the chasms of his lonely
spirit, it flooded past the threshold
of his private world.

Dreamer finally was two men.

One kept his eyes open and chopped
the death ore from its icy mountain
veins. The other closed his eyes
and walked a world whose glory men
never had beheld. Dreamer loved
the world beyond, for there he saw
the only hope of life.

One night during his evening meal,
he began meditating on the great
Invader. Transport was immediate.
Lifeland emerged. The world he loved
appeared around him!

He was not alone. A hand reached
out and clasped his shoulder.

He turned to see a man with royal
countenance.

"I am Ansond. Follow me and you
shall see the measure of your world.
Terra is dying. Beware Elan, and
make him not your Lord, nor wear
his sign upon your chain. Who wears
the sign of Elan bears the mark of
life in vain. For when the War of
Fire is through, Terra shall not rise
again. Come, Dreamer."

Ansond beckoned and Dreamer
moved to his command. The
Singerian's mind spun. Unbidden
flew the gleaming ground. Lifeland
rose up where majesty was found.
At the source of light rose up the
chair of sound.

A thousand, thousand towering feet
of shimmering glass—invisible,
unseen—not even there, yet standing
fast. Ansond fell on his knees and so
did Dreamer. Above them towered
the chair and a voice called out of it:
"Ansond, stand! Come forward!"

Ansond stood and saw the Singer.
Sound swirled. Trumpets lifted
up a fanfare of magnificence. Ansond
knelt before the Troubadour and
touched his forehead to the ground.

Once more he rose and faced the
Crystal Chair and cried the coronation
phrase, calling out with arms uplifted:

"Victory and power! Nobility and
honor to the Troubadour of Life!
Born from the womb of stars! King of
the Crystal Chair! Great symphony
of cosmic melodies of light! Arise
and rule till all glittering night be
born again in splendor.

"Halana to the Singer,
Earthmaker's Living Son!
Halana to the Troubadour
who reigns in sovereign song!
Halana to the planet's star!"

The Troubadour knelt before Ansond,
who took a golden vestment and
laid the rich brocade on the Singer's
shoulders. Ansond took the crown
of life and placed it on the victor's
head.

Once more he approached the Chair
of Glass and brought the Sword of
Ages to the kneeling Prince. He
offered him the hilt.

The Singer stood and raised the
blade.

Ansond and the Prince then faced
each other with their arms raised
to the glass. The Court of
Lifeland sang as one:

"Behold, the galaxy shall quake.
Starstorms will rage where dragons
    groan.
Terra bleeds upon the stake.
The Troubadour ascends the throne.
Halana."

IV

Authentic Messiahs cannot cease
their meditation on vast human hurt
   to heed the pain of nails
   in their own wrists.
Only from the cheaper, little
crosses come the cries of
impaled egoism:
   "Damnation, senseless
   killers! Oh, for a free
   hand . . . and a
   machine gun!"

Ansond climbed to the pinnacle above the Chair of Glass. He stood and called the Phoenix down. Dreamer strained to see the bird hovering in the spangled canopy above the chair. Its shrill scream pierced the battlements:

"Beware Elan,
You sons of man!
He rides the winds
That Death transcends,
And steals all light
To rule the night
of Man!"

Dreamer awoke. Terra's dull materiality emerged. The towering chair dwindled to a post that steadied him. The canopy of stars became the gray reality of cavern walls.

Men were rushing everywhere in panic.

Suddenly he saw the reason for the madness in the mine. From the blackened walls there came a man, half again as large as any miner in the camp. He wore a chain of bronze stars doubled at his shoulders. It ended in a cast-iron world that bore the name of Terra. Through the small, iron globe a sword was run and tiny fissures crowded out on brazen continents and seas. His clothes were dark, coarse and metallic, as though

they had been burnished in some
fiery war between the quarreling
asteroids. His boots were silver
corroded at the soles, for he had
waded bloody fields where Terra's
grudges grew intense from time to
time.

"I am the enemy of fire and knight
of peace," he said. "I hold the keys
that quench and yet release the
fire of Elan. I am the Prince of
Mirrors!"

Dreamer's eyes were now wide open.
No Lifeland this!

"I am the only hope for days ahead.
I've come to turn the world from war
and bless Elan's pursuit of ore that
promises to keep our planet strong
and free. Though the hour is late, the
fire is great that slumbers in these
mines. The spark that we must
quench ignites the times. I guard
and shall redeem the universe that
slumbers just above the waiting
curse."

The magnetism of his words of
warlike peace drew Dreamer. He
wanted to believe yet knew he had to
ask, "But how do you redeem?"

The giant lowered kind eyes and
extended a massive arm in warm
entreaty: "I show you now the portrait
of my hope."

He drew a silvered mirror from his
tunic and held it up to Dreamer's

face: "Here, Dreamer, is the face of
him who sets the planet free."

Dreamer stared and saw his face. His
doubts assailed the doubtful image.
The giant moved on, compelling other
miners to look into his glass. As
each in turn beheld himself, the
Prince of Mirrors cried, "You, sir . . .
and you . . . and you . . . are free with
eyes to see the only hope of man is
men."

When he had shown each one his
face, the Prince put away the glass,
and Dreamer, standing just where he
should to see the Prince's visage in the
glass, saw nothing. The angle of
reflection was correct, but the face
was not there.

The absence of the giant's face only
added to the trouble Dreamer felt
about his words. Invader stirred
within him, and he asked: "But of the
Singer? Is he not the only hope to
stay the War of Fire?"

A hardness moved across the Prince
of Mirrors as he ground out an answer
just as hard: "He is the source of
war and not the stay. Too much blood
already has been shed defending his
small peace. The times are far too
desperate for weak religion now.
It is in men that man must trust
or die."

His face grew softer as he looked upon

the simple miners and smiled at
them in joy. His love seemed pure
and warm and human.

"Men," he smiled in gifted
understanding, "you are the universal
gleam! A beacon on the polished ice
of the Crystal Mountains! You are
the light, unhideable—the hope of
Terra!"

And saying this, he turned abruptly
on his heels and walked away.

Some followed. But Dreamer stayed
to ponder why he could not see the
Prince's image in the glass.

V

"Cassandra, if the world's on fire,
We must save a cup of ashes for
the seed."

T he soldiers of the Emperor marched in rigid columns. Their era had come. The War of Fire began. Each man knew the battle plans and wore the Mark of Elan on the chain around his neck.

The tactic of their treachery was fear. At every city gate they shouted their demand that citizens within receive the Mark. If refused, they called flying Vollkons to raze the villages with fire. The Vollkons numbered only seven but the terror they inspired was beyond all measure. Terra's children sang a monstrous song:

"Seven princes on the spire,
Seven diamonds in the mire,
Seven Vollkons dropping fire
Upon the burning forests.

Who keeps the dragons in their lairs?
Elan, Lord of Ellanor."

Their rhyme was more than nonsense.

Elan kept his ugly pets in frigid eyries in the Crystal Range. Their strength demanded each be chained alone in isolated caves. Even Elan quailed before the Vollkons as a group. He knew the horror they inspired. When he unleashed them, death emerged.

The war began with what was called
the small atrocity.

One misty morning in the Season
of the Center Star, the village of
Varge was waking from the silent
night just passed. Suddenly the sky
broke clear, and through the clearing
fog came screaming Vollkons, giant
claws distended. Canisters of death
ore fell and fire was everywhere.
Children wailed and clung in flaming
death to flaming forms. All life
convulsed and died. Smoke tumbled
thick above the Steppes. Surrounding
cities saw the smoke and feared.

Word of this atrocity spread through
the Steppes. And when the smoke
cleared, Elan ordered his men into
the fear-filled world. At every city's
gate, the citizens remembered Varge
and welcomed Elan's troops. Each
was made to buy the chain of Elan and
wear the heavy medal at his throat.
Elan's bronzed medallion held but
one inscription: "Elan, Lord of
Ellanor."

On the back of every medal was a
silver mirror where each man could
behold the hope of men.

VI

Hell's logic consists in
    preventing murder by
    murdering all murderers.
Heaven's logic greets every
    murderer with grace,
    dying when the time comes
    with a beatific face.

On the evening following the passing of Varge, Dreamer finished his portion of gruel. He walked to one of the abandoned caverns to be with those Singerians who shared the drudgery of Elan's mines.

They met to sing their ancient songs and pray. But this was a special night. On the eve before, a miner had laid aside the seal of Elan and had become unchained. And on this night he waited to receive the Stigmon of the Troubadour.

While some Singerians knelt and sang the Star-Song, the miner felt the joy of wet earth in his palm. He felt a young man trace the Singer's sign upon his brow and heard him say:

"Remember as your hand is stained
That his was crushed and torn by pain
That men of Terra fully know
There is no depth he would not go
To Love.
Earthmaker, Singer and Invader be
The substance of infinity."

After the rite they read passages of hope from THE FINALE. The brazen chain of Elan slept in dust beneath their feet as they sang:

"He comes in power,
Rejoice, the hour of
    jubilee is near.
Lift up the cry
Before we die,
    our Singer will appear."

Finally, they broke the crushed
loaves and ate the Singer's Meal.
While he in reverence held his portion
of the bread, Dreamer closed his
eyes and felt awareness ebbing. He
fought, but Invader swirled in
brightness all around him, sweeping
through his hesitation. The trumpet
sounded and vivid colors blew away
the mist. He stepped back in
astonishment from the Crystal Chair.

Ansond was in armor! Its gilded
surface flashed like fire in the glassy
chair. Dreamer beheld the splendor
of Earthmaker's court of love.

Lightning struck an opaque sphere
resting in the center of the Crystal
Chair. Sound and light shot outward.

"Sorrow comes to Terra!
She wastes in furnaces
    of holocaust.
Nothing can remain.
The planet has nowhere
    now to rest but in
    the ashes of rebellion."

The Phoenix screamed above the
chair:

"Wind shall push the
   flame of war
and drive the smoke of
   suffocation through the world
Till peace has bled a
   deep immortal scar
across the hope of every nation.

Never can there come release
For Terra has despised
Earthmaker's love.
Destruction! Destruction!
The World Hater's fitful
   craze beheaded time and
   slaughtered days
Ignited truth and left the
universe ablaze."

The Phoenix flew upward, shrieking
as she fled:

"Let Lifeland know of Terra's sin,
Let the drama now begin.
Sit, Court of Evermore,
A troupe of players at the door,
Enact the drama of the end."

A trumpet sounded and act one
began.

A small blue ball rolled out in air
and a tiny world was born. Mountain
chains erupted and continents
emerged upon the sphere. Untouched
by any hand the globe revolved.
It turned slowly and unsteadily at
first. Then spun faster, then with
fury. And then it issued fire and
smoke. Then presently it flashed,

exploded into flame and disappeared.

A troupe of actors entered.

One, darkly dressed, strutted onto
the starry stage. He snapped his
fingers, holding out his hand. The
small blue ball appeared again upon
his open palm. Applause filled the
Court of the Glass Chair but the
actor sneered and snapped the fingers
of his open hand. A sword appeared
whose hilt he grasped. He raised
the sword in startling suddenness
and plunged it in the sphere. Blood
washed down the blade and drenched
his hand in red.

Horror filled the court!

"Die, Terra!" he cried out.

The other actors, stunned by this
obscenity, seemed paralyzed. The little
ball convulsed.

The evil actor gloated on the gore,
threw back his giant head and rasped
in fiendish laughter.

Ansond sensed the evil of the drama
and leapt up on the stage. The other
players fell away, and left the
swordsmen face to face.

"Give back the wounded world," the
Golden Knight cried out.

"Never!" shrieked the Black Knight.

"It is Lifeland's greatest love."

"Love cannot save it now!"

The Black Knight threw the bloody globe
into the air and swung his giant sword
completely through the wounded mass.

It split in two.

It burst in flame, and fell.

The swordsman laughed. "Love it
quickly, Ansond, for there is little
left to love."

Ansond dropped his sword and rushed
to grasp the pieces of the broken globe.
He could not let them go. He thrust
the bleeding half-worlds underneath
his cloak and smothered the flame. His
cape was fouled by smoke and blood.

He placed the broken halves together and
carried them reverently to the small
translucent plane before the Crystal
Chair.

One by one the actors lowered their
eyes and passed before the grimy
ball. They cried in one lament:

"Love is done. Hate has won.
Earthmaker's light is gone.
The Night-skies Queen is slain.
Hate has entered Lifeland and
Murdered at the throne of love."

Ansond wept and all of Lifeland with
him.

In crushing suddenness the sword
of the Black Knight pierced Ansond's
armor and sent him sprawling on the
floor.

While the Golden Knight's attention
was on the injured sphere, the
black actor had advanced and swung
his heavy blade into the golden
shoulderguards. The plate had
given way.

Ansond reeled and drew his sword.

"Come, Lord of Hate. Come to the
Blade of Truth!" He spoke to his
dark foe.

Dreamer suddenly recognized the
evil face of the Lord of Hate. The
Prince of Mirrors!

In fury then the titans met.

The lightning flashed each time the
huge swords fell. Twice Ansond fell
beneath the Black Knight's blows.
Each time he quickly rose as the
evil actor approached the small
translucent plane to abuse the
wounded world. Ansond defended it.

Gradually the black actor weakened,
and Ansond delivered a heavy
blow to his helmet. A second strike
fell soundly on the breastplate of
the Lord of Hate.

It split away.

The Black Knight cried out in his
nakedness. The other actors broke
into applause and shouts of joy.

When Ansond saw his enemy
unprotected, he drew back his blade
to plunge it in the heart of universal
hate. But the Black Knight flung
himself over the battlements and
was lost among the stars.

Ansond collapsed, fatigued in
victory. He knew the World Hater
had plunged to Terra furious in
defeat.

He knew that he must follow when
his hands were healed and his
wounded shoulder well enough to
bear the agony of battles yet to come.

The charade was nearly over and
the Phoenix came again:

"Now is the drama ended
As once it was begun.
The same hate wounds
The Golden Knight
That mauled Earthmaker's son.
Rejoice the War of Fire is won
For Terra rolls across the void
And tumbles into sun.
The Singer comes!"

The Singer came. He picked the
broken world from off the shelf and
held it high and shouted out:

"Behold, the old is gone.

The new alone remains.

"The spirit zephyrs drive a healing
    flame.
No world is ever wounded unto death.
Now shall this little globe receive
    her atmosphere,
The Father Spirit's living breath."

Incandescence flashed about his
hand. And when the light had died
away, the world was blue again.

"Terra Two!" he cried.

VII

A God too large to walk in
   human shoes
Has outgrown every hope of
   human use.
And heavy skeptics weighted down
   with doubt
Can never rise to find what
   God's about.

Dreamer found it was time to leave
but feared to go where the drama was
reality in process.

He took the street of monoliths that
led beyond the Chair of Glass. He
crossed the Azure Plain to the Final
Bridge and saw the band of gray
that marked the place where
materiality infringed upon
foreverness.

He paused and looked at the pinnacle
of light. Flying from the spire a
golden banner commemorated
Ansond's wound and announced
that the universe was now at war.

He knew that down the street of
monoliths was soon to come the
army Terra never could withstand.

The promise THE FINALE spoke was
real. Truth would dawn upon the
doubt below. The Singer was coming!
The Golden Knight would not leave
his side till the World Hater had
been conquered. He would fight until
the Emperor was vanquished and
the Vollkons were slaughtered in
the aerie empire of fear which they
inspired.

At the entrance to the bridge he
sat to stare upon the land he loved.
He heard the swelling currents from

the armories of light. The knights
were lost in their own servitude
of grace. The cadence of their anthem
swelled from monolith to monolith
and rang across the Azure Plain:

"The multitudes imprisoned
   soon shall sing of
   greater light.
There are no days more
   splendid than the
   days before the end.
Whose armies can reach
   out with fire? The
   Singer's knights
Soon march with one great
   honor to defend.

He is King, He is Lord,
Singer, Prince and Troubadour."

This scene he loved but could not
stay. He closed his eyes and felt the
shock of transport. A volley of cold
air pierced his soul and he was back
on Terra.

He could hear the voice of the World
Hater preaching in another cavern.

"Man is the hope of men," the Hater
taught. "Behold hope in the glass.
I have taught this great redeeming
hope in every land, beyond the
Steppes of Varge and Thade. In a
hundred cities I have laid the final
hope of men where it belongs. Let
us wear the chain of Elan and sing

across the globe the Anthem of
the Glass."

He paused and Dreamer heard the
miners sing The Hymn of Man:

"The gods are dead, and without
    dread we cheer—
Join hands to reach and cry,
    'We shall not pass!'
We sing in confidence without
    a fear.
We wear one face, behold a
    common glass."

Above him in the upper shafts
Dreamer heard a Vollkon scream.

VIII

A humanist in choking sea
Called for help and presently
Received in full intensity
Advice.
"You must swim, if you would be.
Rescue breeds dependency;
Self-reliance makes one free."
"That's nice!"
He said,
And floated easily
And dead.

When they had finished singing,
the World Hater turned to leave,
then turned back again as if his final
words were more important than
the rest: "I go now into Terra, to
tell all of her people my good news!
I'll preach to every creature the
doctrine of the glass. Terra shall be
saved by this clear, final image of
herself."

One miner, touched by his last
words, cried out, "I too believe.
Give me the chain and glass."

As the Dark Prince handed him the
insignia, he accidentally dropped
it on the floor. As the Dark Prince
reached to pick it up, his silver cape
slid to the side, showing that his
tunic underneath was cut, the fabric
frayed. The gloomy cloth was stained
with blood. A hideous wound was
exposed—a wound that told of
conflict in the skies.

"I saw you there," cried Dreamer.
"You are the World Hater!"

"Where did you see me?" asked the
titan prince, stunned that one could
guess his great charade.

"In the other realm!" Dreamer said.

"Other realm!"

"Yes, even now you wear an injury
ill-gotten in another world."

"You have been too long in frozen
earth, poor man. There are no other
realms. You are the prisoner of time
and space like all the rest of us. Terra
is the only base of life in the lonely
sky. Men are doomed as long as they
pretend to make celestial friends.
This planet's days are done unless
men cease to speak of saints and
singers or trolls and witches in the
sky. Here, Dreamer, behold the
glass and bear our late-come hope—
the mark of peace!"

Dreamer fled in terror from the
room. His flight left those witnesses
in silent stupefaction. The only
sounds were the Black Knight's
labored breathing and the muffled,
far-off cries of Vollkons furious
in their lust for fire and flesh.

Aware they could not leave the
mines, the Prince of Mirrors yet
called out, "Go proclaim the glass
to all of Terra!"

And while he spoke he seemed to
rise and then dissolve like smoke.

Tears came into the eyes of those
beholding his illusive disappearance.
They looked at their faces in the
little mirrors on their chains and
sang again The Hymn of Man.

"The gods are dead, and without
    dread we cheer—
Join hands to reach and cry,
    'We shall not pass!'
We sing in confidence without
    a fear.
We wear one face, behold a
    common glass."

IX

A cosmic coma paralyzed
the star.
The phantom surgeon sutured
tenderly.
A passing comet flashed above
the scar
And light displayed a
planetectomy.

Across the Crystal Range the town of Thade lay sleeping. Like Varge she had refused the Mark of Elan and the counsel of his peace. Her houses were walled in stone and roofed in slate, instead of thatch. She dared to hope this double favor might protect her from the fiery fate of Varge. But flying reptiles screamed just ahead of dawn and fire fell everywhere.

The entire city died.

Fear stalked the living cities.
Elan won the praise of men.
Desperate children sang in terror.

"Where have the little
    cities gone?
The shadow of the
    Vollkons passed.
The flaming air denied
    the truce,
The flying dragons have
    let loose.
The very soil is poisoned
    where
The fire once hung in
    Elan's air."

Terror brought submissiveness.
The planet filled with sheep. The armies now met frail replies and thousands every dawn received the chain of fear. Singerians alone

refused the glass. Many hastened
to the glistening new capital of
Ellanor, the City of Man.

Only in the center of the Empire
were they safe from Elan's fiery
wrath. Everywhere in Ellanor the
Prince of Mirrors preached the
doctrine of the glass and sang The
Hymn of Man.

Dreamer knew it was not safe to stay
within the mines. Mass arrest of all
Singerians was coming and he had
been more vocal than the rest. He
knew he had to flee the mines and
seek the enclave of the capital.

He knew he had to hurry; his
disaffection for the chain and glass
would not be tolerated long. So he
prepared to leave.

His journey would be a desperate
flight up a thousand feet of icy
shafts that passed the Vollkons'
lairs. Once outside the caves of death
the air would be so cold that even
brief exposure would be fatal. Seven
days through icy crags and narrow
ledges would he travel to the Steppes
of Varge and Thade whose ashes
inspired fear.

"Oh, Singer," prayed the Dreamer,
"May your sacrifice
Protect me from the
    Vollkons' fire
And shield me from
    the Empire's ice."

X

Evil finds a ready home
Where beauty is despised
And ugliness enthroned.

The Prince of Mirrors returned
from preaching through the Empire.
On every continent of Ellanor, men
stood enthralled, staring at their
images. "We wear one face, behold
a common glass," they sang.

Elan closed all the temples to the
Troubadour. He decreed that all
who sang the Star-Song would be
imprisoned.

Beneath the Vollkons' lairs and yet
three caves above the praying miner
making ready for his flight, Elan
and the Prince of Mirrors met.
Their covenant was brief.

"You need my doctrine," said the
Prince of Mirrors.

"You need my armies more, if you
would make this world you so
despise sleep in terror and despair,"
said Elan.

"We are in league then?" the World
Hater asked.

"We are. Where is your book of
truth?"

"Here!" the Hater said, pulling
the mirror from his pocket. "Here
is the doctrine by which men
most bend to our control—man's

fascination with himself. In this
small glass is subjugation so complete
it wipes away the universe. As long
as men behold themselves, they
will look no higher, my dear Elan."

"Then I pledge to our new
partnership the fire of fear," the
Emperor enjoined.

"And I... the image of complete
dependency—the face of man."

"I shall hold their loyalty in fear."

"I shall hold their faith in ignorance."

"Together, we control."

"Without a challenge to our
sovereignty."

"I go to burn a city."

"And I to chain man to himself."

The Black Knight tugged at his chin
until his face slipped sideways from
his head and he held his leering
visage in his hand.

The Emperor, too, began to pull his
cheek. His face split away before
his ear and then slid free.

They stood in hideous blankness,
and at length the World Hater lifted
up his face, the masque smiling
horror in his hand. Through its

open lips and eyes the room behind
was clearly visible. It leered and
spoke: "We do agree in common
hate."

"With utter lies I pledge myself,"
said the flattened face of Elan.

Then each man with his empty
hand received the other's face, and
laid it on his vacant plane of flesh
and smiled.

The faces were identical. So were
the hearts.

XI

Prayer is most real when
we refuse to say "Amen."
We most love heaven when
we will not end our
conversations quickly.
Hell is filled with those
who found their "amens"
close at hand.

While Dreamer meditated on
the perils of his flight, his aching
thoughts gave birth to drowsiness
that left him in between his two
realities. Sound shattered his
semiconscious state. The spectrum
of his mind spun, twisted into
colors swirling over gray. The
brilliance left the caverns one full
universe away.

Lifeland was thronged by a sea of
men who waited in eager expectation.
Down the Azure Plain, the Army
of the Singer moved in silence.
Dreamlike they marched in cadence
to a muted drummer who called their
steps precisely.

The Troops advanced between the
stone-faced sentries. Ansond and the
Singer led the legions. When they
arrived at the Great Chair, they
stood and reviewed the passing
troops.

The Phoenix screamed:

"Move back Galactic nebulae.
Hide the shining sea.
Make ready for the War of Wars.
Terra dies.
Leave a black place for her tomb.
Earthmaker will not stay her doom."

And then the Phoenix rose far above

her flaming column and sang the
battle hymn:

"Warfare comes to the
    Plains of Man.
Terra soon shall pass
    away.
Grandeur to the Troubadour!

Raise the praise in gilded
    flame
Till fiery letters etch the
    name
Of love across the waking
    universe.
Singer, Prince of Planets,
Troubadour of Life!"

The army raised their gleaming
halberds in the air and cried an
ancient phrase:

"Earthmaker, Singer and Invader be
The substance of infinity."

In a moment there was thunder
on the Azure Plain.

Dreamer strained to see the coming
horseman. But when the steed was
near enough to see, it rose into the
air above the plain. It soared on
graceful wings and then descended
to the Crystal Shelf before the chair.

One of the knights exclaimed, "It is
the winged Invictrix created in her
splendor to slay the Vollkons of
the Emperor."

A warrior echoed, "Earthmaker's Golden Knight shall fly and slay the seven dragons in the atmosphere of Terra."

Ansond walked to the great winged horse and placed his foot in the stirrup. He swung into the saddle.

At a single command the great steed spread her wings and lunged into the sky. The awesome span would have cast a terrifying shadow had shadows been permitted there.

XII

Come to the court of God
having eyes unwashed with
dreams and you will see
nothing.

Other hoof beats sounded in a
blinding sphere of light that came
in furious speed and thundered
to the Singer's very feet.

Dreamer closed his eyes against
the brilliance and sought to stop
his ears against the sound. A chorus
rose:

"Light-Raider comes from
    that frontier
Where stars unclustered,
    dark with fear
Cower in their eternal night
And beg Earthmaker's steed
    of light."

The light softened gradually.
Dreamer saw Light-Raider,
magnificent and opalescent. From
within his massive torso, flames
shot out in beams that swept the
court.

He had no wings yet he was larger
half again than Invictrix. His bridle
and reins were like strands of raw
color—interlaced illusions. The
saddle swam in shimmering blue-
white hues that undulated in the
towering phosphorescence of the
chair.

A small, bright object rested just
before the saddle on a little plane,

where the mane flowed round it. It was the same blue ball the Singer healed when the dreadful duel of Ansond and the World Hater was done.

Again the Phoenix flew and interrupted Dreamer's meditation.

"Command and Dominion,
    Authority and Grace!
Earthmaker has congealed
    the emptiness of Space.
A new world comes upon
    The Singer's horse.
It is the Hour of the
    Replacement."

A hush fell over Lifeland.

The Singer walked toward Light-Raider with deliberate steps and as he walked he sang:

"Now is complete the Father
    Spirit's dream
Of one small planet sleeping
    in the sun
Of perfect love. The universal
    gleam
Of life as it should be is now
    begun.

Look up! Terra comes made
    new again.
A home for all of those who
    soon will be
Left planetless in space.

Poor hungry men
In sterile fields of
    inhumanity,
I take you in my injured
    hands."

While he sang he took the new world
from before the saddle and held it
high. The Court of the Chair fell
on their faces while the Troubadour
sang out his ballad to the bright
blue sphere.

"I knew your sister world.
    She flew around
Her radiant star without
    disease or pain
Or war, until the new men
    stabbed the ground
Of love. She dies and
    cannot rise again.

My Father Spirit shall not
    let her lie
A grieving vacant deadness
    in the night.
A gallant orbit shall new
    Terra fly
Where her elder sister died
    in flight.

Earthmaker's love is born
    anew
And flies the skies as
    Terra Two."

Light-Raider pawed the ground
and tossed his head and snorted.

He half-reared, then settled on his
great forelegs and knelt. The
Singer mounted. Light-Raider rose.

Taking the reins in his left hand,
the Singer raised the broad sword
in his right and led the army down
the star-swept skyway toward the
Plains of Man.

XIII

Those at Ravensbrück rejoiced
above the rumor that the
Allies were on their way.
Those about to die determined
they would live and strained
upon the housetops to catch
the first glimpse of the
color guard of freedom.

Light-Raider pranced before the
host. Dreamer could see the end
of ranks and files of soldiers. Some
were mounted and some on foot.

He meditated on the hour when
Terra One would give her orbit up
and Terra Two should roll to take
her place.

Whatever Elan did was now of little
consequence. Whatever lies the
Prince of Mirrors told, it mattered
not. The Army of the Liberation
was on its way.

He felt himself beginning to return
and despised the steel-cold air
about him. He fought but could not
hold the brighter world. It slipped
away. He plummeted disconsolate
in gray. Terra One declared to him
her morbid self.

In Dreamer's final hope of hanging
on, he saw the Troubadour astride
his powerful mount. With sword
held high, the Singer passed the
street of monoliths. The gates flung
wide. Beyond the open wall a long
and starless road swung down
between the pale and clustered
light. Even as the cavern walls closed
Dreamer in, he smiled to hear the
army singing through the gates:

"Raise the praise in gilded
  flame
Till fiery letters etch the
  name
Of love across the waking
  universe.
Singer, Prince of Planets,
Troubadour of Life!"

And far in advance of singing knights
the winged Invictrix flew. Above
the starless road she bore the Golden
Knight, whose wounds at last were
healed.

XIV

When comes that final frantic
    marathon
That you did not elect to run,
May there be wild flowers in
    your path,
Pray that your flight be not
    in winter, son.

Dreamer thanked Invader for his presence. He was grateful that his unseen friend would not abandon him now that the hour of flight had come.

Dreamer pulled his coat about him and started down the passageway. At the far end was a shaft that bore a thousand feet of ladders in poor repair. Dreamer's fear of the breaches in the rungs was less intense than his hunger to be free.

Looking up, he saw a tiny speck of light. It was the opening above. The laddered shaft had been a tomb for miners who had tried escape and failed. But youth was on his side and his disciplined young legs would provide strength for the climb.

Three hundred feet above, the walls opened outward on a cavern where the canisters of death ore were stacked. When he passed the arsenal, the sentries' heads were turned away. He moved silently on to chambers above. Cheered by Invader's presence, he thought of Lifeland's army following the winged Invictrix even now down the skyway into Terra.

The spot of light grew larger.

He spanned a treacherous section
of broken ladder bars and passed
another room where torches burned.
Here was the chamber where Elan
and the Prince of Mirrors had lately
traded loyalty and faces.

On he climbed. The light grew. His
legs were now so weary they
trembled.

At last he came to a Vollkon's lair
and ascended through a darkened
corner of its cavern. In the flickering
torches he saw the hideous beast,
far too close at hand, feeding on
a trophy. The smell of fetid flesh was
heavy in the chamber. For a moment
Dreamer thought the Vollkon saw
him. The beast snorted, held up its
scaly head and stared at the ladder
shaft.

Dreamer's heart stopped. Two
sentries, undisturbed, dragged
up another carcass. The dragon
lowered its head and ate. Dreamer
passed on.

Above the Vollkon cavern the shaft
opened on a mountain top. Dreamer
blinked in the brilliant sunlight.
The mountains were alive with
crystalline magnificence. But
Dreamer had no time to admire the
morning. A single sentry barred
his way.

He thought he might slip quietly

behind the guard, gaining the ledges undetected. But as he stepped from the ladder points, the new snow crunched beneath his feet. The sentry wheeled. Dreamer was discovered.

The startled sentry lunged, but Dreamer stepped adroitly to the side. His assailant fell too near the opening of the shaft and only the ladder points could break his fall.

He tried in vain to grasp the wooden posts but his heavy gloves would not let his fingers grasp his hopes. He slid past the posts, clawing helplessly—first at the ladder, then at the air. His scream echoed down the cavern shafts.

Dreamer knew the wail would rouse the Vollkon feeding just below. He hurried down the sunny, icy trail along the ledges which would lead him to the Steppes of Varge and Thade.

In spite of his fatigue his legs found strength. His feet fell firmly on the snowy trail. The morning ledges were steep but comfortable. His fear of pursuit left him. The sentry lay undiscovered at the bottom of the shaft.

By afternoon the descent became treacherous. He sensed the coming of a storm. Then the trail turned

upward, and he had to climb an
outcropping of granite glistening
with ice.

While he hung upon the wall like a
frozen insect, a Vollkon scream
caused his flesh to crawl. He dropped
quickly upon a ledge and pulled his
aching torso beneath a stony
overhang.

Flattened against the wall, he
watched the Vollkon pass. Its scaly
wings throbbed thunder as it flew
toward the Steppes of Varge and
Thade. Dreamer's fear was intense
but groundless. The Vollkon was
not seeking him.

Only when the dragon passed could
he notice that two men rode the
saddle on its neck. He could not
see their faces but the second wore
a black cape that fluttered in the
air and the fabric underneath the
fluttering cloak was frayed.

XV

Conflict is the habit of the ages.
War's amputees sire children eager
to mature and take their bloody
turn at death.

Sir," a sentry said, "there are reports an army is advancing toward the Plains of Man."

"From where?... What cities?" Elan asked.

"From none we know," the guard replied.

"By horse or foot?"

"Both. Horsemen first, followed by an infantry of magnitude."

"Then send the Vollkons. We'll set the cities blazing in their path. The fire will turn the rebels back."

"They are said to be a buoyant army," the sentry offered.

"Buoyant?" Elan seemed puzzled.

"Buoyant!" the sentry repeated. "They sing as they march."

"What about their marching makes them sing?"

"The words, sir, have to do with the crowning of some singer as their universal king."

"The Singer!" cried Elan. "We sealed his gilded temples!"

"We have. Many have been burned."

"And still his superstition lives,"
said Elan in disbelief.

"They sing of him . . . this army.
A general leads them. His horse is
said to be so white that he appears to
be illuminated from within."

"Send the Vollkons! Burn cities
in their path!"

The courier left. From high in the
Crystal Range the Vollkons flew.
East of the Plains of Man twenty
cities burned. Elan was sure the
burning cities would repel the
rebel horde, if such a horde existed.

The Prince of Mirrors was undaunted
by rumors of a coming war. He
preached his doctrine of the glass
in the capital as he had preached
it throughout the troubled provinces.
By now the insignia and seal were
everywhere. Invader forbade
Singerians to accept or wear the
chain. Their disdain of mirrors and
the Prince was widely known.

So persecution came. Those who
refused the mirror and the seal
were put in prison. When Singerians
could obtain bread from the prison
larders, they crushed the loaves
and ate the Singer's Meal. Beyond
the prison walls men smashed
mirrors and laid by the seal of Elan.

Each month thousands cried out to
be unchained and received the
Stigmon as Terra's men had done in
every generation. The prisons
quickly filled and overflowed to
improvised detention centers and
temporary workhouses.

Elan began a curious plan. The
temples of the Troubadour were
many, for Singerians had thrived in
freer days. Elan ordered the gilded
temples converted into prisons:
windows were barred and doors
were bolted. Singerians were
imprisoned where once they were
most free.

Their liberation, Elan said, would
be an easy matter. They had only
to take the chain and publicly profess
the doctrine of the glass.

"Do you believe the Singer lives
on?" said Elan to the Prince of
Mirrors.

"He never lived," the World Hater
replied.

"Yet they say he's coming down some
magic skyway and soon sets foot on
Terra."

"It is the hopeless tale of the
oppressed. Every desperate age
invents messiahs," said the Prince.

"But, were it true..." Elan hesitated.

"Were the Troubadour alive and
general of an alien horde, could he
be stopped with Vollkons or with
armies?"

"I can't say. Men have talked for
centuries about a War of Fire. The
old Singerians have it written in a
book called THE FINALE. But why be
troubled? If the Singer stood now
upon the Plains of Man, would you
surrender or fight?"

"I'd fight!" shouted Elan. "I'd
give him such a thrashing in the
flames..."

"Then I cannot see that it matters
if the rumor's true or not."

"I've burned a score of cities already.
I think it is an idle tale... Still,
thousands have perished to show
him my force, should it indeed
be him who leads this fabled host."

They walked together as they talked
and soon were along the balustrade
above the royal residence.

"Are you afraid, Elan?" the Prince
of Mirrors asked.

"No! Still I must go to the
Plains of Man and see if this army
exists."

A Vollkon winged above the city.
Its ugly head dipped low above

the royal buildings. Its teeth
were parted. The scaly plates of its
abdomen were like corroded brass.
Its six deadly claws were ready
for the bidding of its Lord. Its six
wings brought a turbulence like
thunder.

It came to rest upon a marble finial
and became a gargoyle on the palace
wall grinning at the people far below.

Elan beckoned. The reptile left its
perch and flew to him. He placed
his foot upon a heavy wing and
climbed across the dorsal scales.
He sat down in the saddle on the
grotesque neck. The dragon moved
into the air and soared above the
smoke of twenty cities.

XVI

"Good-bye, cruel world!" his
letter said pinned to his shirt above
the red. His world was cruel. We
wondered why he felt he had
to say "Good-bye!"

Dreamer shivered in the cold. The
moon was bright and he decided to
move rather than sleep in snow
and ice. He knew the Troubadour
was either on the skyway or this very
planet where he trembled in the
cold.

The trail turned down again.
The frozen air stung his face.

By dawn of the second day he knew
he had to rest. Desire had driven
him to fatigue that could no
longer be ignored. The Steppes
were still three days away. But the
worst part of the trip was behind.
The slopes became gentle, the cold
less severe.

He rested in a sunny place. There
was no wind. The morning sun felt
warm. He slept without awareness
of the altitude and cold. His sleep
erupted suddenly in cyclone colors.
The streets of Lifeland were empty.
While his weary flesh slumbered
on the trail, he ran down the Avenue
of Obelisques across the Phoenix's
Court. The gates were open, and the
Army of the Liberation was so far
down the skyway they could not be
seen.

Dreamer was ecstatic! The Singer
might be on the Plains of Man.

A new excitement claimed him. The
invasion might come while he slept
upon the trail.

There was little point in staying
longer. Lifeland did not exist without
the Singer. Dreamer did not rest. He
opened his eyes, stood, then hurried
forward into afternoon.

At sunrise of the third day, he lay
and slept as Invader stirred within.
Sleep had lost desire and would
not transport him to empty streets.

But he had a different kind of dream.
He dreamed of a stable where a black
horse stood waiting while a man in
black clothes ground his sword upon
an emery wheel. The sparks flew in
Dreamer's mind. He recognized the
titan knight who toiled at the
wheel as the Prince of Mirrors.
Dreamer knew that the crude stable
would be his first stop in the capital
of Ellanor, though he knew not
why. Nor was he sure why Invader
showed him this, but he trusted
inner light.

When he awoke, his feet sped with
lightness, as did the days upon the
lower ledges of his flight. Finally,
he came to the Steppes of Varge and
Thade. They had been the first
to suffer in the War of Fire. Now
twenty other cities to the east were
smouldering in death. When Dreamer

saw the carnage, he wept.

Varge and Thade were dead. Whole
cities gone! Only ashes where once
the children played and sang their
rhymes:

"Seven princes on the spire,
Seven diamonds in the mire,
Seven Vollkons dropping fire
On the burning forests.

Who keeps the dragons in their lairs?
Elan, Lord of Ellanor."

"It is a mad existence," Dreamer
thought, "when nonsense rhymes
contain the only sense there is."

He was about to proclaim all life
meaningless, when Invader stirred
him to remember: the Singer was
the only value in a senseless
universe.

Against the morning sun, above the
smoking ruin, rose up the glistening
towers of Ellanor.

XVII

Death is a confirmation of
the believer's creed.
For the skeptic it is discovery,
immense and late.

Elan soared above the smoking cities. Nothing stirred. Death was universal. He gloated on his power. The rumor of the alien army was a farce. Beyond the devastated, blackened earth he saw nothing.

And then his blood ran cold! In the sky ahead—in the sky, where only Vollkons rode—he saw a great winged horse bearing a man in armor. Beneath the flying cavalier he saw the army. For the first time in his reign of tyranny, Elan doubted Elan. He drew the reins on his dragon's head and the reptile turned back across the burning ash toward the Plains of Man.

He knew his fires had been in vain. Burning cities would not stop these aliens. He pondered their origin and feared the flying horse. He remembered old tales that spoke of days of doom and wars of fire.

His bravado ebbed. Was he Emperor? Did he have Vollkons? Was his city safe?

He smiled upon his former fears, then glanced back. The sun on Ansond's golden armor nearly blinded him. He heard the singing host:

"Raise the praise in gilded
 flame
Till fiery letters etch the
 name
Of love across the waking
 universe.
Singer, Prince of Planets,
Troubadour of Life!"

His Vollkon screamed. And—for
the moment—its piercing cry
blotted out the battle hymn below.

XVIII

To break a mirror always brings
 seven years of evil luck,
Unless you have run out of years.

The World Hater knew that Elan had
discovered the invasion. The day
the Hater had long anticipated could
no longer be forestalled. The wound
in his shoulder had not healed,
and the fight would come before it
could.

He hurried through the back streets
to the stable where his horse and
armor waited.

He took a large sword hanging
there and placed the edge against
the emery stone. He pumped the
treadle and the stone revolved.
The steel bled sparks.

His great black horse tossed his
head and snorted. He was ready for
the contest that his master would
soon begin. The Prince of Mirrors
hated Terra and would be glad
to see it burn. Still he wondered
where he would go when the object
of his hate had perished in the
crematorium of war.

He turned the other edge of the
blade upon the wheel. Again blue
sparks leaped into the dark.

The door burst open and the fugitive
Dreamer beheld the Prince's work.

"Can this be? The Prince of Mirrors

preaches peace and sharpens swords!
You cannot win! I left Lifeland six
days ago. Ansond's wounds have
healed and your torn flesh still
gapes. The battle you began with
Ansond you must finish with the
Troubadour himself, World Hater!"

"Why must you use my former
name?" the Prince of Mirrors said.

"It is the only name you ever really
had."

"I'll kill you, Dreamer, and the
world will bless me for your
execution," the Hater spoke with
force.

"Will not Terra think it odd that
he who preaches peace kills those
who disobey the doctrine of the
glass?"

"Look!" the Dark Prince cried.
"Come wear the chain and seal.
Look . . ." he repeated pulling a
mirror from his tunic. "In this glass
lies the hope. Behold your face and
live."

Dreamer tore the mirror from the
titan hand and the giant could
not stay his force. The Hater quickly
grasped the sword and sent it singing
through the air.

"Lower, and you may take my head,"
shouted Dreamer, "but you would

only have it till the morrow. For then death itself will be forever dead, and your spell of terror will be done."

Dreamer felt the inner courage of the great Invader. "Beware, World Hater. I have seen your adversary and he is mighty. And your poor horse cannot withstand Light-Raider. The War of Fire has come. Tomorrow you begin a kind of dying never to be dead. It is your final day to make this world afraid. It is this world's last night. You cannot win!"

"I beat him once upon the wall!" screamed the World Hater.

"Another lie to fit another face! You were beaten then just as you were beaten in the Court of Lifeland. You wear the festered wound. Tomorrow you will lose the third and final time."

The Dark Prince hated him for knowing of his defeats. His face contorted with the hatred he had masked so well in messages of love and peace. The sword blade flashed in the lantern fire.

Dreamer dodged and flung the mirror. It struck the giant in the chest, toppled to the floor and shattered. Dreamer fled into the night.

"He's coming, tomorrow!" he
shouted back into the stable.

The World Hater ground his teeth
and threw down his sword in
senseless anger. It fell into straw.
He winced at the pain in his shoulder
where the wound still seeped upon
his cloak.

Why would the ancient wound not
heal?

XIX

The first sound sleep we ever get
   on earth
We must be roused one realm away.

The Royal Road to the City of
Man ran through death. The Singer
wept as he beheld the charred
etchings of city skylines. Nothing
lived. The Army of the Liberation
rode in silence.

At length, the Singer drew Light-
Raider's reins and slid from the
saddle. Terra Two rested firm upon
the saddle shelf, even as the grand
horse threw his head toward
the sky when the Troubadour
dismounted. He led his horse
through the carnage of Elan's
infamy.

As his boots moved through ashes
that had once been the city of
Aishorihm, his foot fell against an
object in the swirling ash. Around
the wasted torso of a decaying
corpse was the seal of Ellanor. The
tiny mirror reflected only ash.

Aishorihm had died for him who
wished to rule the universe in his
own name. The soldiers closed ranks
silently behind the Troubadour.
Their faces glistened as their eyes
beheld the charred remains of
depravity on Terra.

When he had walked and wept, the
Singer mounted once again. In
somber tones he sang above the

ash of Aishorihm those haunting
words that he had sung so long ago:

"They died absurdly whimpering
    for life.
They probed their sin for
    rationality.
Self murdered self in endless
    hopeless strife
And holiness slept with
    indecency.

All birth was but the prelude
    unto death
And every cradle swung above
    a grave.
The Sun made weary trips
    from east to west,
Time found no shore, and
    culture screamed and raved.

The world in peaceless orbits,
    sped along
And waited for the Singer
    and his song."

The Singer sang no more. The smoke
was too intense, his tears too
frequent.

By noon they passed the zone of
ashes and moved on toward the
capital of Ellanor.

In an instant Ansond soared low
above the troops and cried,
"Vollkons!" He then flew on ahead.
The army halted and watched the
skies.

The evil shadows passed at
stupefying speed. Then fire was
everywhere! The flame scorched
the earth about their feet, then
fled. It blazed on each knight's
armor and yet it did not burn.

The army cheered and soon paid
little heed to falling fire. Their
eyes were turned to the skies, where
Ansond and Invictrix sped to halt
the flying dragons.

Ansond drew his sword to face
the largest Vollkon. Invictrix
maneuvered quickly and in the
first pass Ansond's blade cut one
talon from the beast. The severed
claw, still grasping its canister
of death, impacted on the ground
and scattered flame.

The wounded Vollkon lunged
forward. Invictrix flew at angles
till the sword of Ansond was beneath
the Vollkon's scaly abdomen. He
drove his giant blade between the
armored plates. The dragon's blood
rained down upon the field below,
and then the dying reptile plunged
into the fire storm it had created.

Ansond felt a crushing jolt. The
huge talons of a second beast lifted
him to stare upon its ugly head.
A shaft of pain shot through him
where the dragon grasped his
shoulder. The gaping jaws were
open to devour him. As he passed

the giant eye, he plunged his sword
into the mirrored surface. The eye
split open. The Vollkon screamed
and dropped the Golden Knight.
Invictrix broke his fall by flying
underneath him in midair.

The Vollkon writhed as once again
Ansond drove his sword between
the armored underplates. The second
shrieking beast fell to the fiery
earth.

Two Vollkons yet remained. One,
sensing danger, flew away but
Invictrix overtook it, preventing
its escape. The Vollkon, still
carrying one canister of ore, hurled
it against the harness of the flying
horse. A fiery sphere engulfed
both steed and rider. The light
paralyzed the knight for a moment,
and again the Vollkon tried escape.
Then the globe of flame shattered
as Invictrix bounded into clear sky.

In a spectacular maneuver Ansond
leapt from Invictrix and dropped
astride the back plates of the dragon.
The beating of the scaly leather
wings was deafening. Yet no matter
how the Vollkon tried, it could
not wrench the knight from its
back.

Ansond poised his sword at what
appeared to be a set of shoulder
blades. He plunged the blade
between them and the dragon

screamed and died aloft. Ansond
leaped into the air and once
more alighted in the saddle of his
steed.

The final beast, bewildered by
the rapid death of the others,
prepared to throw its last remaining
charge of ore. Ansond flew directly
at its face and swung his sword
down through the canister the
Vollkon held. It exploded and the
searing flash enveloped both knight
and dragon. Invictrix passed unhurt
through the bright circumference
of fire. But the reptile fell, its
burning hulk colliding hard with
earth.

The Army of the Liberation still in
battle columns cheered and sang:

"Then came Ansond in skies
    filled with fire
And faced the great dragons
    of hate.
In the fiery world where the
    battle unfurled
Their flight came too little
    and late.

"Ansond the Golden has brandished
    his light
And the beasts of war have not
    fled.
Fire burns on his sword and the
    Black Knight
Shall die where his dragons
    have bled."

And then they sang the magnificent
hymn of the hosts:

"Warfare comes to the
    Plains of Man.
Terra soon shall pass
    away.
Grandeur to the Troubadour!

"Raise the praise in gilded
    flame
Till fiery letters etch the
    name
Of love across the waking
    universe.
Singer, Prince of Planets,
Troubadour of Life!"

XX

"The sky is falling!"
said Henny Penny.
"No, poor bird, it
only seems that way
when the earth is
rising to higher
levels of righteousness
and love."

Elan could not believe it. Four Vollkons had perished in the encounter. In the days that remained he had to mobilize his legions. They were at battle stations on the Plains of Man, facing the east in numbers so abundant that their armor seemed a silver ribbon around the walls. Alert, the soldiers waited and watched the road to catch sight of the alien horde. They scanned the skies to catch a glimpse of Ansond's horse. But the bleak day ended and nothing yet was visible.

The three remaining Vollkons had been busy carrying the canisters of ore from the Crystal Range to the central armory well inside the City of Man. It was clear to Elan that the capital was the destination of the Singer's troops and the likely site of conflict. When all the ore had been transported, the Vollkons perched on the eastern wall above the troops of Ellanor like a crown of evil on a doomed city.

Fear gnawed the capital. The city had been sealed. The gates were bolted and the drawbridge drawn.

Inside the city those who wore the chain and seal heard rumors that an alien army stretched around the planet.

Who were they? Where was their
kingdom? Who were the flying
knight and singing general? And
most plaguing of all, "Why could
Vollkons not destroy them?"

The Singerians inside the city
were jubilant. "He comes!" they
said as they met each other in the
dismal streets.

At the beginning of the second day,
while the soldiers gathered in
formation on the plains, the Prince
of Mirrors rode through the streets.
For the first time he was on his
horse. He wore a helm, breastplate
and sword. His eyes searched every
crowd he met. He sought but could
not find Dreamer. The Death Stallion,
a black steed who matched the
giant's hulk, was ominous.

"Dreamer is in the city," the
Prince of Mirrors said to Elan, who
showed small concern. "Elan! He has
escaped your mine in the Crystal
Mountains and has crossed the
Steppes of Varge and Thade on foot.
He is here now in the capital telling
everyone of the military exploits
of the Singer and his knights. He
is preaching in the streets that
Ellanor will perish in the War of
Fire. He dismays those who wear
the seal and chain. He cries that
all must now repudiate the doctrine
of the glass."

Elan sensed the fury in the voice.

"His bleak words," continued the
Black Knight, "set the city in dismal
doubt about your ability to defend
it. Let us now impound all Singerians
not already in our prisons and put
them to death!"

"It is the only way," agreed Elan,
somewhat absently.

"Now!" demanded the Dark Prince.

"Yes, now. There is very little time,"
Elan said.

The Prince of Mirrors rode to the
armory and made the announcement.
The sentries arrested everyone
who did not wear the chain.
Singerians were ferreted from homes
and alleyways, and placed in an
old building near the armory.

The Prince of Mirrors watched
the arrests but still did not see
Dreamer. When all had been
collected, the Hater rode his horse
through the guarded doorway of the
temporary compound. When they
saw him in their midst, the
Singerians began to chant, "He
comes! He comes! He comes!..."
Their voices grew in volume till
the Black Prince could not stand
the roar.

Then they began the chorus:

"The Prince of Dragons
   soon must fall
Before the Prince of
    Planets."

The World Hater had no tolerance
for their music. He had heard it
through too many centuries. He
once had hoped to grind the music
into silence. Now the hour was late
and the music rose around him
with foreboding. The Death Stallion
pranced uneasily amid the mob.

The Prince of Mirrors reined the
horse so sharply that it reared into
the air and wheeled upon its
haunches. He swung his long sword
in each direction and the hooves
of his steed fell again and again.
The brandished blade cut
indiscriminately. Then quickly
he departed.

Dreamer had been arrested with
the others. Yet he had not been
discovered by the Dark Prince.
From the shadows of the makeshift
prison he beheld the massacre and
wept. He embraced an old and dying
woman, careless of the gore clotted
on her wrinkled face.

"He comes!" he said to her.

"He comes!" she said through
pain. Her smile froze into silence.

The Invader swirled hope through

the darkened room like hurricanes
of light. His brilliance pushed
back the gloom. Joy washed down
their faces. "He comes!" they cried.

The dead were moved to the center
of the room as the Singerians
voiced the words of THE FINALE they
had left too long unsung:

"He comes in power,
Rejoice, the hour of
    jubilee is near.
Lift up the cry
Before we die,
    our Singer will appear."

XXI

Take your visions.

Give me photographs.

The book of visions always has
   blank pages, for the mystics
   never can agree on exactly
   what they saw.

The album's filled with photographs
   where lens and light and silver
   nitrate record the moments as
   they were.

A steady light may be observed.

A flash, however brilliant, is
   debated.

Three hours before the dawn,
the stone face of the prison house
crumbled. The roof blew away.
The prisoners stood at once to their
feet. Through the devastated walls
they saw the starry sky. One star
began to grow, flooding the
sleeping city with its light. It
settled ever closer until it came
into their very midst.

"He is here!" shouted Dreamer.

The glare softened into friendly
incandescence and then into a glow.

Invader had gathered the harsh
light around him and swirled it ever
faster until the two great lights
converged in a blinding supernova,
then softened once again.

A great horse emerged from the
brilliance and the Troubadour
dismounted.

The prisoners fell upon their faces.

The Singer with one hand held
Light-Raider's reins and with the
other palm he lifted up the face of
a young man.

"It is over," he smiled. "I have
come!"

The lad leapt upright and embraced
the Troubadour. The Singer threw
his arms around the youth and kissed
him.

An older child ran to embrace the
pair.

At once the assemblage converged
upon the trio. Their joy was
immense.

Dreamer had never been so happy.

The long-awaited Prince had come!
Then Dreamer saw the woman who
had died in his arms. She was alive
and reaching to the Troubadour. So
were all who had been slain. The
Singer knew the old woman as he
knew them all. He walked to her.

"Will I ever have to die again?... It
was so ... so ..."

"I know how it is to die," he smiled.
"But dying is over now."

"Come with me," the Singer called
out to the other prisoners. They
followed him outside. The sentries
looked yet never saw them. Light-
Raider and the Singer led them
through the streets. Invader's light
moved ahead of them. The streets
were swelled with people from each
quarter of the city. Singerians
came—smiling, running, dancing
through the gates.

There were many in the streets
and yet the army of Ellanor did not
rise to quell the unseen midnight
riot.

Near the gates, the Troubadour
swung back into his saddle. Invader's
light glinted from his crown and
he raised his swordpoint to the city
gates.

The gates opened and the drawbridge
lowered itself across the moat.

The liberated prisoners sang
boldly and advanced through the
gates. Even as they passed Elan's
troops, they sang without fear. The
sleeping Vollkons never noticed
them or heard their songs:

"The Golden Age has dawned
    upon the grave of time
And we are free!
We lay aside the chains of
    our humanity.
The Singer comes to save the
    remnant of the age.
The gates fling wide!
The banner waves above the
    Troubadour of Life
Astride a steed of light!

"He comes! He comes!
The blind can see!
The halt march perfectly!
The prisoners are free!

"He comes! He comes! He comes!
Lift his name, his universal
 love.
Spread majesty in light above
 the stars,
For we are free!"

The Army of Liberation heard the
captives singing and the soldiers
erupted in an anthem of their own.

The realms met.

Lifeland and Terra at last were one!

In the daisied meadow soon to be
a blazing field of war the liberators
and the liberated sang as one:

"Raise the praise in gilded
 flame
Till fiery letters etch the
 name
Of love across the waking
 universe.
Singer, Prince of Planets,
Troubadour of Life!"

And the spectacle of life began.

The Army of Liberation fell upon
their faces as the Troubadour
approached. The liberated captives,
too, bowed themselves to the ground.

The Singer sat resplendent on his
horse and looked upon the union
of the ages.

He lifted up his glittering sword
to the great glass chair so many
light years distant:

"Father Spirit," he cried
   into the night sky.
"It is done. They are yours,
Earthmaker, the Magnificent!
These are the evidence that
   only faith is sane,
And never more shall freedom
   wear a chain.
Hate is vanquished. Joy has
   won!
Now ends the flight of
   Terra One.
And Terra Two shall fly the
   newer sky
In love."

While every knight knelt, Terra
Two rose gently in the air from the
shelf before the saddle.

There boomed above the plain a
gallant chorus rising somewhere
deep in space. It was an old, old
song and the tune reached hauntingly
again to touch the Father's face.

And Terra Two began to grow. It
spun in midair, rose high above
Light-Raider as the Star-Song echoed
through galaxies.

"The melody fell upward
   into joy
And climbed its way

in spangled rhapsody.
Earthmaker's infant stars
   adored his boy,
And blazed his name in every
   galaxy.''

The plains of Ellanor were suddenly
baptized in a golden incandescence,
nearly as luminous as that which
lit the Azure Plain of Lifeland.
Each of the newly liberated fell in
double columns that flanked a
blinding aisle down which the Singer
passed. Dreamer found himself in
the long column on the right.

He waited till the Troubadour passed
in front of him. Like others who
preceded him in the column, he
knelt. The great sword touched his
shoulders, and the cool blade on his
naked flesh was the confirmation
that he was now part of the Army
of Liberation.

When the Singer had passed,
Dreamer stood with the firmness
of a victor. He stiffened with
military air when he realized he was
dressed like all the other soldiers.
The silver mail hung upon his arms
and shoulders. The Symbol of the
Singer was raised in bronze relief
above his breastplate. His sword
lay flat within the scabbard that
rested against the greaves, and his
gauntlets were tucked behind his
studded belt.

What had happened to the woolen
rags he had worn only moments
before? He didn't know, but he wore
the new dignity well. He knew that
tomorrow he would fight the War
of Fire. His hand rested firm upon
his sword and he smiled.

XXII

Light is never given
while we fear the dark.

When dawn came, the Army of Liberation drew their swords and began the advance. They marched in silence toward the enemy columns stationed by the wall. Elan, in the saddle of a Vollkon laden with the ore of death, advanced to meet the enemy. His bridled reptile released the canisters. Fire fell everywhere, but the Army of Liberation marched on.

Elan feared.

The unbridled Vollkons flew again to the armory and returned to hurl more fire. The heat grew so intense that the forests near the Plains of Man ignited. Sheets of flame swept in waves across the land and licked the base of the fortress walls. It looked as if the entire globe would burn.

Elan made a tactical error. He decided that the Singer must be killed to stop the onslaught.

Astride his great dragon Elan dived toward Light-Raider who did not bolt.

Giant claws grasped for the Troubadour but could not sweep him from his horse.

Then suddenly the Vollkon looked
toward the sky and screamed.
Ansond closed on him. The Golden
Knight recalled a ploy he had
used in earlier attacks and sliced
through the canister which Elan's
dragon grasped. Fire engulfed both
beast and rider.

As the saddle girth collapsed and
the searing flame rushed over him,
Elan wailed in terror. In separate
moments yet almost one, Emperor
and Vollkon hit the earth.

Two Vollkons remained. One
wheeled and confronted winged
Invictrix in the air. Wildly its six
great talons ripped the air. Invictrix
barely kept beyond the reach of all
its savage claws. Each way the horse
flew, the beast turned in the air to
face Ansond and fight. The roaring
Vollkon almost deafened those
below. The reptile opened its deadly
jaws to grasp the horse's wings.

Below the screaming skies, the battle
ranks began to close. Along a
hundred-mile front, sword clashed
on shield. The wail of dying men
continued through the day. Above
the din of war echoed the cries of
dragons in the air.

By afternoon the Vollkon had
begun to tire. Invictrix circled it
until the sun fell full into the
monster's face. The reptile's glazed

eyes spoke its death ahead of time.
Its wing beats slowed and finally it
settled toward the earth. It could
not rise although it longed to do so.

Invictrix and her rider watched
the beast descend. It hovered for
a moment above the thickest combat,
then fell the few remaining feet.

The men of Ellanor moved back to
give the dragon dying space. Its
great leather wings fluttered like
a crippled gull. Its claws dug into
the bloody earth among the corpses
of the fallen soldiers. It whimpered,
groaned and gasped. Then died.

The dragon's slow, painful death
unnerved the men of Ellanor. They
had reason to fear. Elan was dead.
Terra was aflame and the fire had
spread to the capital. The gates
were now ablaze.

Ansond turned to the final Vollkon.
The beast, knowing it was the last,
had lost its heart for war. It would
not fly. It perched like a great stone
gargoyle on the palace armory
where the canisters of death ore
were stacked in pyramids.

As Invictrix flew close, the Vollkon
toppled backward, scattering the
deadly piles.

It could not fold its wings. Spasms
shook its ugly head. Froth

poured above its forked tongue.

Seized by desire to end its existence,
it brought a merciful conclusion
to the war. Grasping a canister, the
Vollkon tore the frail shell until
it burst. In an instant fire shot high.
The whole armory detonated. Flame,
growing in intensity, collected in
a golden ball and settled on the city.

Terra was ablaze! Hate's final grudge
against Earthmaker's love was
holocaust.

Dreamer, turned Avenger, struggled
to find the Prince of Mirrors in the
burning city. He was confused by
all the flame. The streets were filled
with the fallen, and the buildings
were in ruins. He sought the stable
where the Dark Prince had sharpened
his weapon for the conflict.

A cloud of dense smoke blew across
the small lane where Dreamer
walked. A burning timber crashed
ahead of him and exploded in a
shower of sparks whose light was
smothered by the soot and darkness.

He fought the smoke and, shielding
his face against the heat, he stumbled
through the hot mist. When Dreamer
drew his arm back to breathe, the
Prince of Mirrors stood directly
in the burning way.

The Hater grinned and drew his sword.

XXIII

Materiality: A blessing all its own.
Spirit-Demons play in fire
hoping for cremation.
In the terror of their immortality
they envy dying men.

In the days prior to the Liberation, Dreamer would have been terrified by the leering Hater. Now he was amazed that the aggressor's grin left him unafraid. The Hater's sword was twice the size of his, but he drew his own blade and stepped the thirsty distance to his foe. The Hater swung. Then the smaller swordsman hurled his steel in a direct arc that would have hit the Hater's armor. The sound of clanging steel resounded through the streets. Each stalked the other. Again their blades resounded as Dreamer slowly weakened.

Suddenly Ansond bolted through the smoke, calling to the Hater, "Come! Leave the Dreamer! Your wounded shoulder still seeps my grudge."

"Not before I finish with this miner," the Prince of Mirrors cried. He followed his defiance with a question, "Is Elan dead?"

"The planet's dead!" cried Ansond, "and Elan with it. He fell in flame from a slaughtered Vollkon."

"He died wearing my face," mused the World Hater, ". . . but no matter, I have his."

"Terra died because it wore your face," Ansond interrupted.

Gesturing to the flames the Hater cried, "Look, Ansond! I have laid to rest Earthmaker's hope and smashed his finest work of art. Behold the power of hate!" He laughed.

Dreamer watched the unfolding conflict. Suddenly he was dazzled by blinding intensity. Light-Raider bolted through the wall of flame. Ashes formed whirlwinds beneath his hooves. The Singer came.

"It is your final moment!" called the Singer.

"Perhaps," the Dark Prince said. "The planet burns and the flames spread. Perhaps the seas themselves shall erupt in flame," he laughed.

"Indeed they will," the Troubadour agreed. "Hate sometimes has a fiery end before it is absorbed in love."

The old antagonists faced each other as the Troubadour continued. "My Father-Spirit loved this place and the men he made to live here. "Now . . ." He seemed choked by the declaration. "Now . . . both his world and men are gone."

"I told you I would win," sneered the World Hater. "I warned you

at the wall. The fight was fair. Now
see the ash can of your artistry."

"You have not won... Look!"
Ansond sent his mount through
the wall of flame. The fire fell back.
Low in the night sky flew Terra
Two. It had grown since it floated
upward from the saddle shelf a few
hours earlier.

The Troubadour smiled. "In only
three hours comes the midnight of
this planet. Terra One will die!
But even as it falls the sky will be
filled with the growing hope of
Terra Two. It is a world that you
will never enter, World Hater."

"You cannot kill me, nor control
me. I go to any world I wish. I once
brought civil war to Lifeland itself.
Have you forgotten?" The Prince
of Mirrors sneered at the world
growing above the flames.

Invictrix soared abruptly back
through the flames and settled
suddenly. Surprised, the Dark Prince
stumbled backward and fell
ingloriously to the charred ground.
He looked up at Ansond who trailed
a long chain of heavy links.

Light-Raider pawed the earth and
it opened in an awesome rift. From
the great scar the Hater could hear
the moaning from the Canyon of the
Damned.

"No . . . no!" cried the World Hater.

The Singer leapt from Light-Raider. The ancient struggle began again in fury. Hate tore at Love for the remaining hours. Terra Two loomed larger and larger until it filled the sky. Close to midnight, the World Hater in desperation flung his sword at the Troubadour.

The Golden Knight now entered into the struggle. He grasped the discarded sword and wielded it to split away the Hater's torn and dented armor.

Evil stood naked.

Ansond knew he could not put an end to the evil prince with the sword, for they had both been made to live forever. So he took the chain and wound it round the Hater's wounded body.

The Hater cursed the Singer and his Golden Knight and poured his scorn on Terra Two.

Dreamer beheld the final moments of the ancient struggle. The World Hater would live forever but never move again. He would hate but never enter Terra Two.

Invictrix nudged him toward the great rift. Over and over he rolled.

At the edge of the crevasse Invictrix
nudged him one more time. He
tumbled into the abyss and
plummeted away.

The ground closed.

Dreamer followed Ansond and the
Troubadour back to the waiting
army. The soldiers like himself
were all unharmed.

The War of Fire was over.

The Singer led the Army of Liberation
back upon the skyway.

At midnight the two worlds collided.
Terra one split away and then
dissolved. Terra Two rolled on in
youth.

XXIV

An old astronomer clasped his
   protégé and said,
"If Polaris dies tonight,
Be assured some greater light
Will take its place."

Ansond guided his mount above
a mountain range. He saw the
spires of the City of the Troubadour.
A lovely city without walls, for
walls though not forbidden were
forgotten. In worlds where evil has
not come walls never come to mind.

Invictrix skimmed a sunlit tower
and flew down to the plaza where
the children played. The steed
alighted. Ansond walked through
an arched portal and saw the Singer
sitting with his lyre. He saw
Ansond and rose to meet him.

The two embraced.

"Earthmaker is sovereign love!"
said Ansond.

"The music of the universe!" agreed
the Troubadour.

"Halana to the Father-Spirit!"
cried the Golden Knight.

"Come with me!" the Singer said.

They walked to the Plaza of Peace.
In the center of the square a
sphere of bright transparent glass
rested on one crystal's very point.

In the center of the sphere was a
world about the size that Terra Two

had been the day she rode into the
final battle of the War of Fire.

"It is Terra One—a replica,
exact and scaled," the Singer said.

"Forever sealed?" inquired Ansond.

"Forever," agreed the Troubadour.

"And we can never hear the anguish
from its center?" The Golden
Knight seemed troubled.

"Never. There shall be silence
where the Dark Prince writhes in
chains."

"He is small indeed to live in such
a tiny world as this."

"His is a dwindling point of death
within a growing universe of joy."

"Come," said the Singer. They
walked again.

Soon they came to a grand reliquary
on a distant ivory causeway. There
was a cube of glass and deep within
a replica of the Great Machine of
Death.

"Why keep this?" Ansond asked.

"It was the only hope of Terra One.
Those who walk this newer world are
here because I chose to die down
there between the gears and ropes."

"What was it like to die?" the
Golden Knight asked.

"Be grateful you shall never have
to know."

The Troubadour looked thoughtfully
away. "When it was over, I held
a new relationship with men. Even
Terra One died. Death does not
matter." The Singer gestured to
the glistening world of Terra
Two. "Dying is not final, only life."

Ansond looked at the scars of death
still marking the Prince's hands.

"You are the Singer, Prince and
Troubadour!"

There was music all around them in
the air.

They sang the Star-Song, and far
above the Crystal Chair, their
music drifted outward on the
universe.

"Earthmaker viewed the sculptured
   dignity
Of man, God-like and strident,
   President
Of everything that is,
   content to be
His intimate and only earthen
   friend."

HALANA.